Theodora Hendrix and the Snare of the Shadowmongers

JORDAN KOPY

Cover illustrations by Chris Jevons
Interior illustrations by Lisa Hunt

WALKER
BOOKS

THEODORA HENDRIX and the SNARE of the SHADOWMONGERS

For my sister, Tappy Jordan,
who marches to the beat of her own drum
and who reminds me to have the courage to
march to the beat of my own.
J.K.

First published 2022 by Walker Books Ltd
87 Vauxhall Walk, London SE11 5HJ

2 4 6 8 10 9 7 5 3 1

This book has been typeset in Berkeley Oldstyle Book

Printed and bound by CPI Group (UK) Ltd, Croydon CR0 4YY

British Library Cataloguing in Publication Data:
a catalogue record for this book is available from the British Library

ISBN 978-1-4063-9263-0

www.walker.co.uk

PROLOGUE
The Last Secret

Oh, good, you're here. I was afraid you weren't going to make it; I fully expected your parents to forbid you from joining me on this next adventure, our most daring yet.

You see, your parents – those Masters of Mystery, those Keepers of Truths, those Eaters of Snacks After You've Gone to Bed – are afraid. Terrified, even: they don't want me to tell you this last secret, the greatest of them all. As far as they're concerned, I should never have told you that monsters exist in the first place, and they're simply furious that I have introduced you to a great many of them since then. Indeed, your parents would be a whole lot happier if I just kept my mouth shut. But unfortunately for

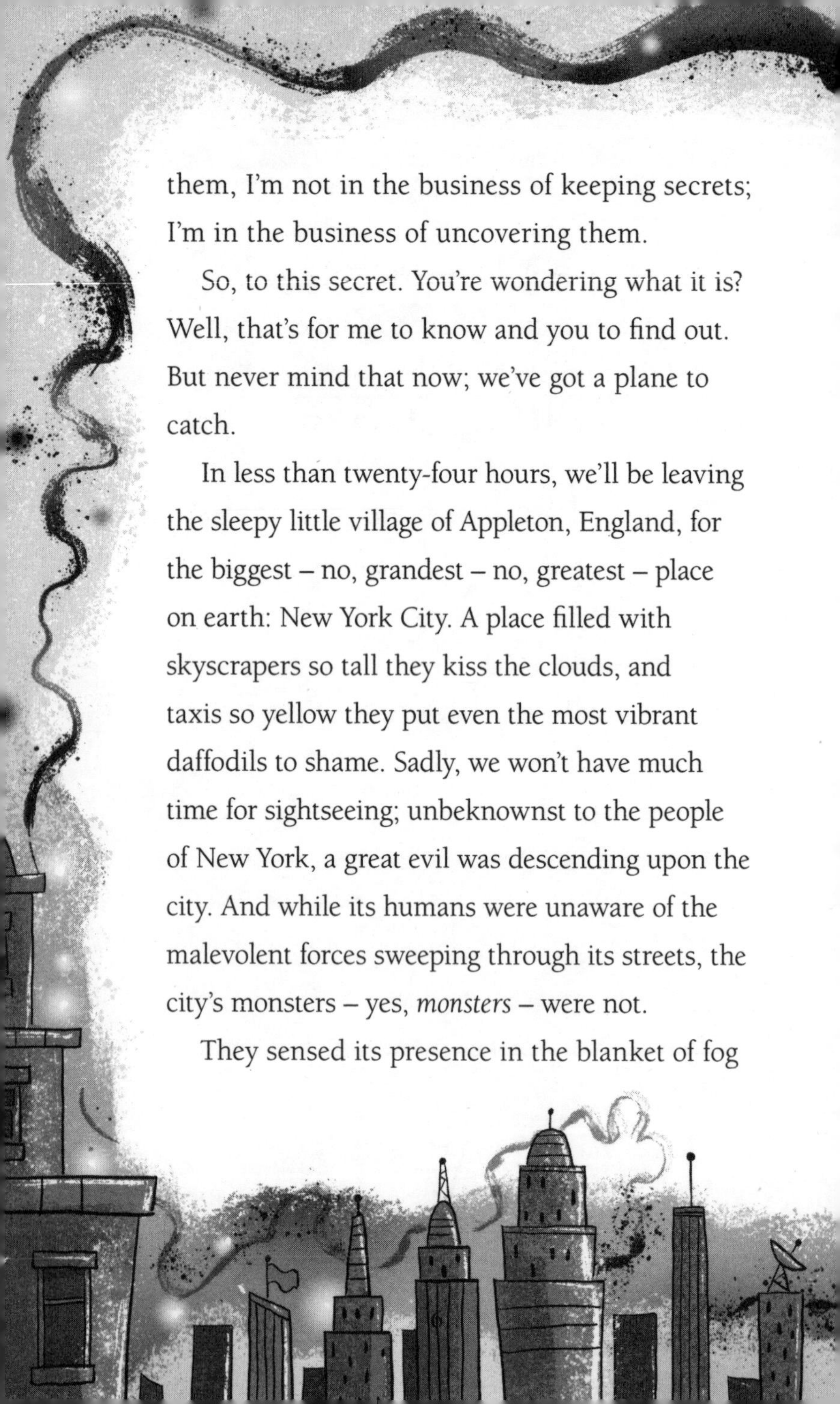

them, I'm not in the business of keeping secrets; I'm in the business of uncovering them.

So, to this secret. You're wondering what it is? Well, that's for me to know and you to find out. But never mind that now; we've got a plane to catch.

In less than twenty-four hours, we'll be leaving the sleepy little village of Appleton, England, for the biggest – no, grandest – no, greatest – place on earth: New York City. A place filled with skyscrapers so tall they kiss the clouds, and taxis so yellow they put even the most vibrant daffodils to shame. Sadly, we won't have much time for sightseeing; unbeknownst to the people of New York, a great evil was descending upon the city. And while its humans were unaware of the malevolent forces sweeping through its streets, the city's monsters – yes, *monsters* – were not.

They sensed its presence in the blanket of fog

that had settled over the city, the dense mist that clung like cobwebs to their skin and hair and fur. They felt it in the sharp bite of the wind, in the frigid temperatures that turned their noses red and their fingers blue. They saw it out of the corners of their eyes: a dark, shapeless *something*. And though this something – whatever it was – vanished upon closer inspection, it was there nonetheless, skulking in the shadows, hiding in closets or under beds, waiting for the perfect moment to strike…

Some three thousand miles away, the members of the London Monstrous League of Monsters (MLM for short) were blissfully unaware of the wickedness across the sea. They bustled about the MLM mansion, packing their bags for their upcoming trip to the Big Pumpkin. (Why do you think *we* are going there in the first place? Keep up, Junior Agent – things are moving fast!) And while the monstrous inhabitants of 13 Battington Lane were looking forward to their travels, not one of them was more excited than the mansion's sole human resident: Theodora Hendrix, who simply couldn't wait. Having recently faced down an evil hag, battled a murderous mummy, and outsmarted a clever inspector and her even cleverer pet rat, she figured she was due a nice, relaxing, pizza-filled holiday. (New York City is famous for its pizza, in case you didn't know.)

Little did Theodora know that her holiday wouldn't be nice, and it definitely wouldn't be relaxing (though there would be pizza). Instead, it would be filled with monstrosities not seen since the days of the Egyptian pharaohs, when monsters ruled the land and humans lived to serve – whether they liked it or not.

Agent Charles Holmes,
Eye Spy Monster Agency

The Witching Hour

It was a cold, clear night. Hundreds of diamond-like stars twinkled overhead, studding the endless stretch of black that was the sky. And if you happened to be in the village of Appleton, England, and if you happened to look up at those inky heavens at just the right moment, you might see more than stars. If you were lucky – or perhaps *un*lucky – you might see a figure sitting astride a broomstick, speeding past the moon.

In case you didn't know, the best spot for witch-watching is a graveyard: witches, like most creatures of the night, are drawn to such places. Perhaps that was why the villagers gave a wide berth to the strange, spooky space that was the Appleton cemetery.

"They say it's haunted," Mrs Next Door would say, sipping her tea.

"I don't care what they say," Mr Down the Road

would scoff, giving his glass of whisky a swirl. "There's no such thing as monsters." He wouldn't mention that just the previous evening, he awoke with a start to find the silvery spectre of his late wife rocking in the chair beside his bed, her knitting needles clicking just as swiftly and loudly as they had in life...

"Even so," Mrs Across the Street would chip in, "that place gives me the creeps."

Mrs Across the Street had the better measure of that most haunted place, for at any given time there were any number of spooky things prowling about it. In fact, one such thing, a zombie named Georgie Hendrix, was approaching the Appleton graveyard at that very moment. It is here that our story begins.

Georgie ambled into the cemetery, easing the gates open with a creak. A blur of tan – Georgie's very best friend, a masked vampire-cat called Bandit – streaked between his legs. The cat's lamplight eyes were fixed upon a particularly old headstone. Three centuries' worth of rain, wind and snow had smoothed the stone, but if you looked closely, you could just make out the name *Georgie Hendrix* etched into the marble.

Bandit sprinted ahead, coming to a stop beside Georgie's plot. "Meow!" he cried. Now, as you very well know I can't speak cat, but I think Bandit must have said something along the lines of, "Georgie, I think someone's been messing with your grave!"

The zombie's rotting eyes swept across the graveyard. Bandit was right: someone had disturbed his plot. His mouldering, splintering coffin had been dislodged from the dirt, revealing a hole – no, tunnel. Someone must have dug it, but who? And more importantly, why?

"Eurga," Georgie said, the drooling slash of his mouth twisting into a frown.

"Mew meow?" Bandit asked. In this case, I think he meant, "Are you saying that you think whoever's behind this didn't break *into* your grave, but *out* of it?"

Georgie nodded.

"Meow?" Here, I think, Bandit's meaning was quite clear: *"Who?"*

Georgie pointed to the base of the headstone. There, barely visible between the overgrown weeds, was a fingernail. It was long and sharp and, judging by the sickly shade of green, full of fungus. Bandit's fur stood on end; he thought he knew to whom it belonged…

"Eurga," said Georgie, confirming the feline's fears. "Eurg."

"Meow," Bandit sighed in agreement, reluctantly taking the filthy fingernail in his mouth.

The pair exited the graveyard, heading for the sprawling, crumbling mansion that sat on top of the hill just over yonder. Wordlessly, they picked up their pace. There was no time to waste – oh, this was *bad*…

You're wondering why the appearance of a fungus-filled fingernail had so alarmed the monsters? So am I.

The old-fashioned alarm clock on the nightstand read 12 a.m. but ten-year-old Theodora Hendrix was wide awake. She was sitting on the floor in the middle of her bedroom, which looked as if it had been struck by a tornado: clothes and hair ribbons were scattered everywhere, while shoes spilled out of the wardrobe like a smelly rubber river. A suitcase sat in the middle of her bedroom floor, along with a briefcase the size of a postage stamp. But Theodora could not claim credit for this bit of packing, as the briefcase belonged to Sherman, the talking, top-hat-wearing tarantula.

"Theodora," called a voice from above. "You *still* haven't packed?"

It was Sherman, helicoptering down from a crack in the ceiling on a strand of spider silk. "You haven't packed at all," he chided, all eight of his milky, monocled eyes sweeping across the messy room.

"I know," Theodora groaned, running a hand through her tomato-red hair. "I just can't decide what to bring. What's the weather like in New York, anyway?"

"Freezing, I expect."

"Guess I don't need a bathing suit, then," she said, tossing hers aside.

"No, but some of these jumpers would do nicely."

With Sherman's help, Theodora finally began to make progress. Just then, there was a knock at the door. In walked a mummy, and not just *any* mummy. This mummy – aptly named, well, Mummy – just so happened to be one of the world's fiercest warriors. Her small but powerful frame was wrapped from head-to-toe in soft, snowy linen offset by a shiny gold crown. And though they weren't visible, Theodora knew that two bejewelled knives were hidden inside her bandages, waiting to be called into service.

"What are you still doing up?" asked Mummy. "It's well past midnight."

"Just finishing packing."

"Then let's close that case and get you tucked in. If you're late for school tomorrow, Ms Frumple won't be happy."

Theodora crinkled her nose at the mention of her head teacher. They had never got on, but over the past few months their relationship had deteriorated greatly – probably because Ms Frumple blamed Theodora for ruining her plans to make some major (and awful) changes at school. Theodora and her friends had protested, and ultimately the school governors had sided with them. Ms Frumple had taken to ignoring Theodora ever since. Mummy wasn't pleased with this behaviour (which was, in her opinion, unbecoming of an educator), but Theodora didn't mind. In fact, in many ways she found it to be an improvement.

"Do I have to go to school tomorrow?" asked Theodora, slipping between her pumpkin-patterned sheets. "It's the last day of term, so we won't be learning anything."

"School is only to be missed if you're feeling ill, or if there's an emergency."

Theodora scowled.

"Careful," Mummy said lightly, smoothing the

crease between her brows, "or your face will freeze like that." (Have your parents ever said this to you? I figured. Well, I can assure you that it *won't*; your parents are just trying to distract you from whatever they did to cause you to pull a face in the first place. They're sneaky like that.)

"It'll be over before you know it," said Sherman, swapping his top hat for a sleeping cap. "Then we'll be on our way to New York City!"

"And Dexter and his family arrive the day after we do," Mummy reminded them, referring to Theodora's best human friend, Dexter Adebola. "Mrs Adebola has invited us for dinner at her sister's apartment. Can you imagine? A dinner party with actual *humans*!"

Mummy was right – it would be fun to hang out with Dexter while they were away, and she only had one more day of school to get through. Cheered by the thought, Theodora finally settled back against her pillows.

"Sorry to interrupt," called a deep, mournful voice from the doorway. A voice that could only belong to the mansion's skeletal butler, Helter-Skelter. "But Dracula's called an emergency MLM meeting." He held up a bony finger, from which a small, furry bat was hanging upside down.

It was Mummy's turn to frown. "Did he say why?"

The butler shook his head.

"I'd better go." Mummy sighed. "Night, Theodora. Night, Sherman."

Theodora waited a beat for the sound of their footsteps to fade, then whispered, "What do you think that was about?"

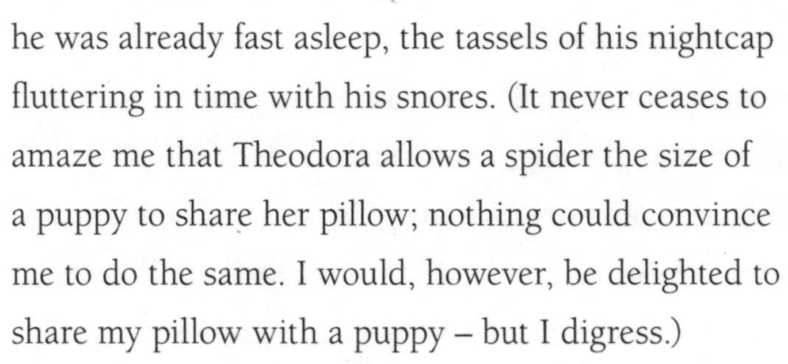

But Sherman didn't reply; he was already fast asleep, the tassels of his nightcap fluttering in time with his snores. (It never ceases to amaze me that Theodora allows a spider the size of a puppy to share her pillow; nothing could convince me to do the same. I would, however, be delighted to share my pillow with a puppy – but I digress.)

Theodora sighed. She supposed she'd have to wait until tomorrow to hear Sherman's thoughts on the matter. She burrowed beneath the covers, eyes fluttering closed for what would turn out to be one of the last nights of good sleep she would enjoy for quite some time...

The Zombie's Tale

As Theodora lay dreaming of buildings so tall they vanished into the sky and lights so bright they blotted out the stars, the monsters of 13 Battington Lane filed into the mausoleum, which doubled as the MLM meeting room. Located deep in the belly of the mansion, the torch-lit chamber was dotted with white marble tombs and featured a lone worktable littered with bits of parchment and the odd goblet. Nailed prominently to one stone wall was the MLM Charter. As you already know (and if you don't by now, you *really* haven't been paying attention), the charter listed three rules:

MONSTROUS LEAGUE of MONSTERS
CHARTER

1. Keep monsters hidden from humans
2. Protect humans from bad monsters
3. Help bad monsters become good monsters

In case you do need a refresher, I'll remind you that all monsters must follow these rules; those who don't risk Headquarters' wrath, including imprisonment in the Darkest, Dankest Prisons of Transylvania. Of course, most monsters are sensible beings and as such are perfectly happy to abide by the Charter, but there are some who are *not* so sensible: monsters like the sinister hobgoblins who have a taste for human flesh and who reside in cemeteries – including the very one that Georgie and Bandit had just left.

Speaking of Georgie and Bandit, they had just arrived on the scene, eager to share their discovery. They joined Dracula (yes, *the* Dracula), the vampire, pacing back and forth; Mummy the mummy, watching the vampire's progress with increasing concern; Wilhelmina, the witch, sipping from a mug of pink bubbles; Grimeny Cricket, the buggy bringer of death, scribbling in a tiny notebook with an even tinier quill; Bon, the bonadoo (a creature with the body of a hare and the mane, tail and teeth of a lion), munching on a carrot that, judging by the clods of dirt still clinging to it, was freshly pulled from the earth; Marty, the werewolf, tapping his foot impatiently (this was prime moon-howling time); Gabe, the ghoul, lurking in the shadows; Figaro, the operatic ghost, practising his scales; and Pimms, the poltergeist, bobbing towards the ceiling.

"That's everyone," called a rather odd-looking monster with a pumpkin for a head, mismatched eyes (a star and a crescent moon respectively) and a body made of vines twisted into the shape of a man: Sir Pumpkin-de-Patch the Fourth, of course. (What a mouthful, eh? But as you know, you can just call him Sir Pumpkin-de-Patch.)

"Then let's begin," said Dracula, clapping his cold, bloodless hands together. "I'm sorry to have interrupted your evenings, but we've had some worrying news. Georgie, Bandit, the floor is yours."

"Eurga," said Georgie. "Eurg eurg. Eurga eur egua. Eurg."

"Are we to understand," Mummy began, "that someone dug a tunnel beneath your coffin and used it to break *out* of your grave?"

"Eurg," he confirmed.

"Buuuut whooooooo would dooooo such a thinggggggggggggg?" sang Figaro.

In reply, Bandit leapt onto the table and spat out the nail he'd carried from the graveyard. It hit the wood with a thwack, gleaming in the glow of the torchlight.

"Is that a *fingernail*?" drooled Gabe from the corner.

"Disgusting," Marty grunted.

"Meow," Bandit said importantly, lifting his chin. "Mew – mew! – meow. Meoooow!" In this case, I think Bandit said, "We found this horrible fingernail – it tastes awful! – by Georgie's headstone and we think it belongs to Hilda!"

This announcement was met with stunned silence. No one liked thinking about Hilda, that most wicked of hags. A former member of the London MLM, Hilda had been banished after she had turned bad: not only had she plotted to overthrow Headquarters in a failed attempt to bring monsters out of hiding, but she had also tried to kidnap Theodora, whom she had wished to keep as a pet.

"I suppose it fits," mused Grimeny Cricket, breaking the silence. "After all, the last time we saw Hilda was when she was being pulled into Georgie's grave by a hobgoblin…"

"She can't have survived the hobgoblin's attack, can she?" wondered Sir Pumpkin-de-Patch. "They're very dangerous."

"So is Hilda," Marty countered. "You oughta know that by now, Pumpkin-head."

"Don't call me Pumpkin-head! My name is—"

"What do you think, Mummy?" Dracula interrupted, lest Sir Pumpkin-de-Patch and Marty began an argument as they had during the previous meeting. (Marty's cubs had dug up Sir Pumpkin-de-Patch's vegetable garden; the latter hadn't been pleased.)

Mummy carefully tucked a piece of loose bandage behind her ear, considering. "I think they're right: Hilda must have survived the hobgoblin's attack underground, dug a tunnel to escape and broken out of Georgie's plot."

At this the others erupted, arguing the merits of her words.

"Quiet. QUIET!" Dracula yelled. "If Mummy thinks Hilda is back, then Hilda is back; she's rarely mistaken about such things."

"And even if she was, *you'd* still agree with her," said Pimms slyly, waggling his ghostly eyebrows and making kissy sounds.

"And just what is that supposed to mean?" Dracula sputtered.

"Never you mind," said Wilhelmina, glaring at the poltergeist. "Besides, the question is not whether or not Hilda survived; I daresay she did. The question is: why has she remained underground for so long?"

"Sheeeee muuuuuuuust beeeee uuuuuup tooooooo soooooomething," sang Figaro.

"And what if that something involves Theodora – what if Hilda goes after her again?" worried Bon, his half-eaten carrot all but forgotten.

"Theodora only has one more day of school and then we'll be on holiday," Mummy said. "Hopefully by the time we're back Hilda will be long gone."

"I'll beef up security just in case," said Marty, the Monster Head of Security. "And I'll ask Bob and Sally to keep an eye out too," he added, referring to the great stone gargoyles who guarded the mansion's roof.

"Good thinking," Dracula said. "If there's nothing else, I'll bring this session to a close. Meeting adjourned."

The monsters drifted out of the room in twos and threes, until only Dracula, Mummy and Wilhelmina remained.

"I have a bad feeling about this," said the witch.

"So do I," Mummy admitted.

"We'll be in New York tomorrow," Dracula said soothingly. "Hilda won't be able to get at us there – and more importantly, she won't be able to get at Theodora."

Oh, how very wrong he was.

The Prisoner's Flight

The next morning, the shrill shriek of the alarm clock woke Theodora bright and early. She rolled out of bed, glaring at a still-snoring Sherman; unlike her, he didn't have to go to school so didn't need to rise at this most un-monsterish hour.

Yawning, Theodora shuffled down the hallway, lined with a dozen snoring suits of armour, and into the bathroom. She washed her face and brushed her teeth but didn't bother combing her hair: it was as snarled as a vampire-mouse's nest, and she was simply too tired to deal with it. With another yawn, Theodora returned to her room and dressed for school.

"Breakfast is ready," said Mummy, popping her head in.

"Thanks," Theodora replied, scowling as she

adjusted the severely starched collar of her uniform. "I just need to do my reading."

"Quickly, please – you only have half an hour before school."

"OK," she said, moseying over to her desk and picking up a pack of cards – *torat* cards, to be exact.

Surely you know all about torat cards by now? No? Tsk, tsk. Fine, I'll explain, but you'd better pay attention because this is the very last time I'm going to do so.

Torat cards, like tarot cards, offer insights into the reader's life. Indeed, they're similar except for a few key differences (and *no*, I'm not just talking about the way they're spelled). Firstly, torat cards can only be read by the child for whom they were made. If your interfering grandpa Bill or your meddlesome Auntie Em tried to read them, they wouldn't be able to – they would just see a regular pack of playing cards. Secondly, torat cards are created by the elusive rata-tat-tats, fashionable ladies who wear oversized sunglasses and bright red lipstick.

Recently, Theodora's deck had revealed a third, rather unusual trait: the cards had mysteriously changed, their images altering to feature Hilda and her monster-in-crime, a skele-crow (a skeletal monster that can take on the fleshy form of an animal, in this case a crow). After the MLM had defeated the wicked pair, the cards had reverted to their usual selves. But then in October, when the horrible Inspector Shelley and her even more horrible rodent assistant had been staying at the mansion, the cards had changed again – at least, *The Seven of Magpies* had.

Originally, the card featured six birds at the bottom and one at the top. But now, the ink of the lone magpie had faded so that only a faint outline remained. Theodora had no idea what to make of this. (Neither do I, for that matter.) Wondering if it would appear in this morning's spread, she shuffled the cards, randomly selecting three. The first, representing her past, featured a golden-haired woman in flowing robes of powder blue.

"*The Lady*, as usual," she sighed. "Secrets. Mysteries. The unknown." No matter how well or how often she shuffled the deck, Theodora always selected this card first – which

I suppose is fitting: to this very day, no one knew who her human parents were, why they had abandoned her in a graveyard, or what had become of them since.

Theodora flipped over the second card, representing her present, to reveal *The Seven of Magpies.*

"Pilfering and thievery. Uh-oh," she muttered, noting that the lone magpie had now vanished *completely.*

She threw down the third and final card, representing the future. It featured a black-haired woman sitting upon a throne in the middle of a lush, verdant forest.

"*The Empress,*" Theodora said, intrigued. "Love. Nurturing. Motherhood. That's new."

"Theodora," Mummy

said, reappearing in the doorway. "You've got twenty minutes to eat and get to school!"

"Sorry!" she replied, hurriedly slipping the pack into her pocket and following Mummy out of the room and down the hallway. They paused at the top of a marvellous ivory staircase inlaid with hundreds of human eyes. The steps themselves were *moving*, rippling like waves (one of the mansion's many excellent defences – more on this later).

The motion ceased as they approached, allowing Mummy and Theodora to skip down their length. "Morning," Helter-Skelter said as they entered the kitchen.

"Morning," Theodora replied, settling herself on a stool at the counter.

"I thought we'd have a bit of a treat to celebrate the last day of term: pancakes!" he grinned, tipping three piping hot, fluffy pancakes onto her plate.

"Awesome!" she replied. Pancakes for breakfast was definitely better than cereal and much tastier than the hated hard-boiled eggs. (Yuck.) She was halfway through the stack when Sir Pumpkin-de-Patch barrelled into the kitchen.

"Mummy, come quick!" cried the Monster-Gardener-in-Chief, dripping leaves as he waved her over.

"What is it? Did the cubs dig up your plants again?"

"No," he said darkly. "It's the dungeons."

A shiver ran down Theodora's spine; as far as she knew, the dungeons were empty save for a single prisoner: a skele-crow. And not just any skele-crow… *Hilda's* skele-crow. To think that this most foul fowl was somewhere in the mansion made Theodora's skin crawl, but Marty had assured her that the bird was kept under strict surveillance. But, Theodora thought, the pancakes turning to sawdust in her mouth, if the dungeons were so secure, then why was Mummy jumping to her feet at the mere mention of them?

"You're to finish your breakfast and go straight to school," Mummy told Theodora sternly, following Sir Pumpkin-de-Patch from the room.

Theodora waited until the sound of their footsteps faded, then leapt off her stool. Between last night's emergency MLM meeting and whatever was happening in the dungeons, it was obvious that something major was going on – and she intended to find out what.

"What about your pancakes?" Helter-Skelter yelled after her retreating form.

"Save them for me!" She hurtled down a hallway dripping with cobwebbed candelabras, slowing as she reached the end: she needed to stay far enough behind Mummy and Sir Pumpkin-de-Patch that they wouldn't notice her, but close enough to keep track of their movements. Theodora had never actually been to the dungeons and didn't know exactly where they were located: given her penchant for being in places she wasn't meant to be (ahem, the Ancient Curse Breaking Room), the MLM thought it best to keep their location secret. Personally, Theodora thought this was overkill, but then the monsters were generally overprotective.

Keeping her distance, Theodora followed Mummy and Sir Pumpkin-de-Patch into a bare little room that housed the Wall of Shame (a series of portraits featuring bad monsters, including Hilda, the skele-crow and a mummy named Abrax). The room was normally empty except for three heads – yes, *heads* – sticking out of the wall: a ruby-eyed rabbit, a sly-looking fox and a deer with gilded antlers. Right now, though, it was filled with monsters.

Mummy, Sir Pumpkin-de-Patch, Wilhelmina, Dracula, Bon and Marty were huddled together. It was the werewolf that drew Theodora's eye: he was lying on the floor, unconscious, an egg-sized lump pushing through the skin of his skull. She bit back a

gasp, wondering what – or who – could have injured a monster as ferocious as Marty.

"Mummy," said the rabbit in a high, reedy voice, "thank darkness you're here."

"What's happened?"

"It's the dungeons," wheezed the fox.

"What about the dungeons?" asked Mummy, with the air of one struggling to maintain her patience.

The Heads exchanged a look.

"See for yourself," said the rabbit.

"Very well," Dracula agreed, moving to stand before the deer. "May I?" he enquired.

The deer considered his request, then nodded.

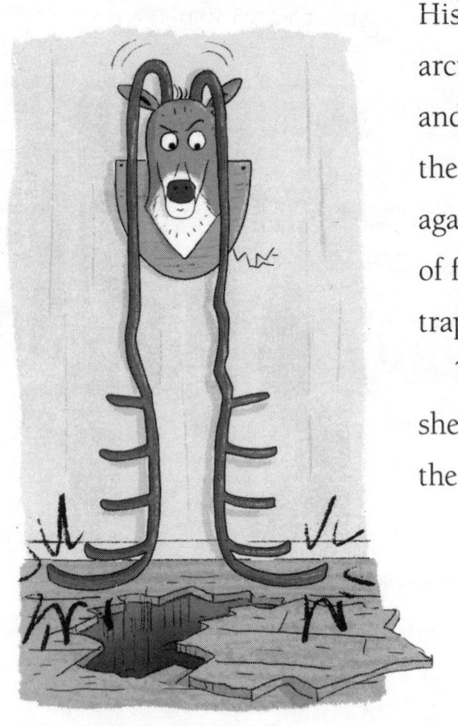

His antlers began to grow, arcing over his delicate head and lengthening towards the floor. They tapped against the wood. A section of floor fell away, revealing a trapdoor.

Theodora's jaw dropped; she knew that if you stroked the wall in a particular spot, a secret door leading to the music chamber would appear, but she had no idea the room held *another* hidden passageway. (Though I'm not sure why she was so surprised: a mansion as haunted as 13 Battington Lane was bound to have *lots* of secret passageways.)

"Thank you," said Dracula. Then, without further ado, he leapt down the hole.

"Shall we?" asked Sir Pumpkin-de-Patch.

"Yes," said Wilhelmina. "But someone ought to stay with Marty."

"I'll do it," offered Bon.

"Thank you," said Mummy as she, too, vanished into the floor.

Sir Pumpkin-de-Patch and Wilhelmina followed.

Theodora waited until the top of the witch's tall, pointed hat had dropped out of sight, then bounded into the room.

"Theodora!" the rabbit said in surprise. "Shouldn't you be at school?"

"Yes, she should," said Bon with a thump of his foot.

"It's the last day of term," Theodora said, carefully avoiding Marty's sprawled form as she edged towards the trapdoor. "We won't be learning anything new anyway!" She was desperate to see what was going on, and there was no way she was turning back now. Before Bon and the Heads could say any more, she jumped into the hole.

Down, down, down she went, flying along a slick-smooth slide until she landed with an "oof!" on a pile of pillows – no, not pillows, she realized as her eyes adjusted to the light (or lack thereof), but stuffed animals.

Thinking this was a strange addition to a dungeon, Theodora wondered if she was in the right place, but the thought was fleeting: she heard a clanging sound, like chains being rattled. Dusting herself off, she edged towards the sound. She soon found herself standing in a corridor comprised of jail cells. Two massive, mossy boulders were positioned outside the furthest cell. No, not rocks – trolls! Trolls who attended the MLM Reform School run by Mummy. (You'll recall ***Rule Number Three:*** *Help bad monsters become good monsters.* That's where the Reform School comes in; for additional details, see my previous works.)

What, Theodora pondered, could take down monsters of this size? Deciding she'd rather not think about it, she crept past their prone bodies, peering into the cell they'd been guarding to see the MLM gathered around a cage – a *birdcage*, to be exact. It was empty, swinging creakily on a rusted chain despite the lack of breeze. Black feathers – *crow* feathers, unless she was mistaken – were scattered about the packed dirt floor.

"The skele-crow," Mummy said incredulously. "It's gone!"

"But how?" asked Dracula. "The cage was padlocked, and there's no light in here – he couldn't have transformed into his skeletal state..."

"It's obvious, isn't it?" Wilhelmina replied. "He had help. And there's only one monster we know who's mad enough to break into an MLM house..."

The Anca Feathers

"Hilda," Mummy said flatly.

Theodora drew a sharp breath. Hilda, *back?* She couldn't be! Could she? Of course, if she was, it made a great deal of sense that she would steal the skele-crow – he was her monster-in-crime, after all… And then Theodora was struck by a thought: was this the theft of which *The Seven of Magpies* had warned? She shivered.

"It all fits!" Wilhelmina cried, referring to the events of the previous evening (although Theodora didn't know this). "The last time we saw Hilda, she toppled into Georgie's grave. Then last night, it was discovered that Georgie's grave had been disturbed and a fingernail – a hag's fingernail – was found at the scene of the crime. And now this morning, the skele-crow – a known associate of Hilda's – has escaped from our dungeons. It can't just be a coincidence!"

"I'll notify Headquarters," Dracula said heavily. "I'm sure they'll want to increase their own security in case Hilda's planning something bad..."

"We'll need to keep a close eye on Theodora," said Sir Pumpkin-de-Patch. "What if Hilda makes another grab for her?"

"Then I'll be ready for her," said Theodora bravely, stepping out from the shadows.

"Theodora! Didn't I tell you to stay in the kitchen?" asked Mummy. "You're not supposed to be down here!"

"Must not have heard you," Theodora said blithely. "Besides, isn't it better if I'm prepared?"

"She's got a point," Dracula allowed.

"Perhaps. But there's nothing to be done now – Hilda's not foolish enough to hang around."

"Which begs another question," said Wilhelmina. "How did Hilda get in?"

The monsters shook their heads; the mansion was supposed to be impenetrable.

"Maybe Marty saw something? Hopefully he's come round by now. Let's ask him."

They exited the cell, reviving the trolls on the way with a wave of Wilhelmina's wand and soon arriving back at the large pile of stuffed animals that had softened their collective landings.

"How do we get back up?" Theodora asked, eyeing the slide.

"The Anca feathers," explained Sir Pumpkin-de-Patch, picking up one of the stuffed geese. "Up, please," he said, as if expecting it to reply. To Theodora's surprise, it *did*, startling her with a great *honk!*. An instant later, a real, live goose appeared in its place.

The goose preened itself for a moment, then plucked a single feather from its coat, which Sir Pumpkin-de-Patch solemnly accepted. The bird flew out of the gardener's arms, flapping to the floor. With another *honk!* it returned to its previously inanimate state.

Sir Pumpkin-de-Patch lifted the feather into the air. "Up," he said in a loud, clear voice. With a whoosh he was gone, flying *up* the slide.

"Light as a feather," Wilhelmina murmured. "Grab a goose, everyone."

"Theodora, I want you to go straight to school," Mummy said as they emerged into the bare little room a few moments later.

"But what about Marty?"

"I'm fine," grunted a voice from the floor. The werewolf was sitting up, clutching an icepack to his shaggy head. "But I've got a wicked headache…"

"Did you see anything, Marty?" asked Theodora, sidestepping Mummy.

"Nope."

"Heads, did you see anything?"

"Afraid not," the rabbit replied. "Someone must have turned off the lights; it was black as pitch."

"We need to call another MLM meeting," Dracula decided.

"Agreed," said Wilhelmina.

"Agreed," said Bon.

"Agreed," said Theodora.

"Oh, no," Mummy said, gripping her firmly by the shoulders. "You are going to school!"

Theodora opened her mouth to argue, but, catching sight of Mummy's thunderous expression (sort of how your big sister looks when she catches you "borrowing" her sweater without first asking permission), wisely did not reply. She allowed Mummy to steer her back into the kitchen, gratefully accepting a napkin full of pancakes from Helter-Skelter. Swinging her knapsack over her shoulder, Theodora gave Mummy a kiss goodbye and headed up the road to school under her watchful eye.

"Meow," Bandit said by way of greeting, winding himself between Theodora's ankles.

"Morning, Bandit. Sorry I'm late, but you'll never guess what's happened," she said, filling him in on the walk to school.

Five minutes later, Theodora heaved open the doors of Appleton Primary with some difficulty: it was only 9 a.m. but between staying up late last night and this morning's excitement she felt very tired indeed.

I am sorry to say that the rest of the day would be just as exhausting: in a few minutes' time, Theodora would come face to face with none other than Ms Frumple. I am *very* sorry to say that Ms Frumple wouldn't be pleased with Theodora's tardiness, or her attitude, or her – well, let's just say there was a lot Ms Frumple wouldn't be pleased with. And I am *even* sorrier to say that the head teacher had an awful – no, terrible – no, horrific – punishment planned for Theodora as a result. A punishment so horrible that, upon hearing it, Theodora thought she might actually prefer to face Hilda…

The Assignment

Theodora shoved the now-empty napkin into her pocket, exchanging it for the note Helter-Skelter had written explaining her tardiness. Armed with the slip of paper, she entered the Year Five classroom.

"You are very late indeed," said her teacher, Mrs Dullson.

"Sorry, Mrs Dullson," replied Theodora, handing her the note. She made her way to her desk, which was right next to Dexter's. Small, reedy and exceptionally good at chess, Dexter was the only human in all of Appleton who knew that Theodora lived with a family of monsters. Or so they thought…

"E-everything OK?" he muttered, surveying her through his thick, black-framed glasses.

"Not really," she muttered back. "The monsters think Hilda has returned."

Dexter, who'd once met the hag and knew first-hand how terrifying she was, let out a squeak like a mouse being trodden on. Before he could react further, the door swung open to reveal the head teacher, wearing a supremely ugly sweater the exact colour of cat sick.

"Morning, Mrs Dullson. The secretary has just informed me that Theodora Hendrix was not present for registration?" she enquired.

"She's here now," Mrs Dullson replied.

Ms Frumple's narrowed gaze swept across the classroom, finally settling upon Theodora. "Come with me, Ms Hendrix."

Theodora and Dexter exchanged a worried look; this couldn't be good.

"Good luck," whispered Ella Vargas, a studious girl whom Theodora and Dexter had recently befriended.

"Give her heck," added Billy Ellis, a boy who occasionally picked his nose when he thought no one was looking – and whom Theodora quite liked despite this unfortunate habit.

Theodora straightened her hair ribbon, then followed Ms Frumple out of the room. They did not speak as they walked down the empty corridor, with only the click-clack of Ms Frumple's shoes to punctuate the silence.

"Come in, please," said Ms Frumple when they reached her office.

Theodora trudged inside, slumping into her usual chair while Ms Frumple primly settled behind the desk. The head teacher didn't speak, surveying Theodora with interest as if she were a puzzle that couldn't be solved.

"Well, Ms Hendrix," she said at last, "you have the dubious honour of being my most frequent visitor."

"Erm," said Theodora, unsure of what to say; she had a feeling "thank you" wasn't the response Ms Frumple was looking for.

"I'm sure you're wondering about the reason for today's visit?"

"Well, I was late..."

Ms Frumple arched a brow.

"*Ma'am,*" Theodora added hastily; Ms Frumple had warned her on numerous occasions that she expected to be addressed as "ma'am" at all times.

"Your tardiness this morning, while unacceptable, is not why I called you here. Today's issue is purely academic: Mrs Dullson told me that you still haven't handed in your end-of-term project, due two weeks ago. Well?" she prompted when Theodora didn't reply.

"Well, what – ma'am?"

"Where is your project?"

Theodora avoided the head teacher's gaze. The truth of the matter was that she hadn't done the project, which was to make a family tree.

In case you're wondering, a family tree is a chart that shows a person's lineage, listing their parents, their grandparents, and so on and so forth. You can imagine the challenge Theodora would have in making such a chart, given that she had been adopted as a baby by a family of monsters; she couldn't exactly glue pictures of Mummy and Dracula to a posterboard. Nor could she trace her ancestry, given that she knew nothing about her human parents.

"I don't know, ma'am," she finally replied.

"Perhaps a three-day suspension is in order," Ms Frumple said gravely.

Theodora perked up at the thought. Although she knew Mummy wouldn't be pleased – and she would most certainly be grounded – the idea of an additional three days off school was not altogether unpleasant.

"An *in-school* suspension," Ms Frumple clarified, a crocodile-smile on her thin, colourless lips. "With me."

Theodora's mouth fell open in horror: a three-day suspension with *Ms Frumple*? She honestly couldn't think of anything worse. "Oh, please," she pleaded, "please don't! I'll do the project, cross my heart and hope to live!"

"I believe the expression is, 'cross my heart and hope to *die*'," corrected Ms Frumple. (Shows how little she knows about monster-isms.) "I suppose I could give you a detention instead ..." she considered.

Hardly daring to believe her luck, Theodora said, "Thank you, ma'am!"

"... so long as you hand in your project on the first day back in January."

"But it's Christmas!" Theodora exclaimed. "My family's going to New York. I won't have time."

"I suggest you make some," Ms Frumple said severely. "Is that clear?"

"Crystal, ma'am."

"Then you may go."

Theodora was on her feet and out of the office faster than a rabbit fleeing a fox. She was halfway down the corridor when she walked right into Mr Johnson, the cantankerous old caretaker. *Oof!*

"Oy!" he cried, waving his ever-present mop at her.

"Watch where you're goin'!"

"Sorry," Theodora said, dodging the sudsy droplets spraying from the mop. "I didn't see you."

But Mr Johnson didn't seem to have heard her, and continued to rage for several minutes. Theodora sighed, waiting for his rant to end; it was going to be a *long* day.

At breaktime, Theodora wasted no time filling Dexter in on all that had passed in Ms Frumple's office.

"M-making you do h-homework over the holidays?" he asked, shaking his head sympathetically.

"I don't know what I'm going to do."

"You'll j-just have to set aside some time and g-get it done," Dexter said reasonably.

"That's not what I mean. How am I supposed to complete my family tree when my family is made up of monsters? And I don't know anything about my human parents."

"Oh," Dexter said sheepishly. "I uh, g-guess you c-could, you know, m-make it up?"

"I suppose." But the very thought made Theodora uncomfortable, for reasons she couldn't quite explain even to herself.

"It'll all work out," Dexter assured her. "Besides, we're going to have so much fun in Manhattan, you won't have time to worry about some dumb assignment. Just you wait. There's pizzerias on every corner – you can eat pizza every day!"

"I think I'd feel quite sick if I ate pizza every day," said Ella, sidling up to the table, nose buried in a book (as usual).

"Hi, Ella," said Theodora. "Ready for the break?"

"Oh, yes," she replied.

"I just opened the invitation to your party," said Dexter as Ella took a seat. "But your birthday isn't until January – why'd you hand them out so early?"

Ella shrugged. "Just figured sooner was better than later, what with the holidays and all."

"Makes sense. Well, you c-can c-count me in! Will your grandpa make one of his famous chocolate cakes?" Dexter asked hopefully.

Theodora didn't hear Ella's reply; her insides were squirming as if a bunch of worms had got loose in her stomach. Ella was having a party? A party that Dexter was invited to but that she, apparently, was not.

"Hope so," said Billy, sauntering over. "Chocolate's my favourite." (Mine, too.)

The worms in Theodora's stomach grew into snakes; *Billy* was going to the party too? She hadn't even known that Billy and Ella were friends. Sure, they all sat together at lunch (a welcome change from the days when Theodora used to sit by herself), but she'd never really noticed Billy and Ella hanging out on their own. Or was it possible that the whole class had been invited, except for her?

"I don't care what kind of cake it is as long as it's got lots of frosting," Dexter said dreamily. "What's your favourite kind, Theodora?"

Thankfully, the bell rang before Theodora could reply; she had no desire to discuss Ella's party any further. She was feeling a bit – well, stupid. She'd thought she and Ella were friends. New friends, sure, but friends nevertheless. But obviously she was wrong.

As Theodora took her seat, she didn't think she'd ever been more ready for a holiday. Of course, she didn't know of the horror-ble (see what I did there?) danger awaiting her in New York.

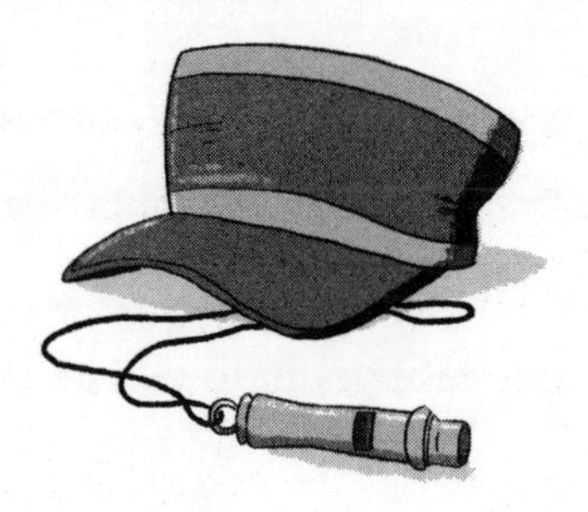

The Glass Express

Theodora crossed the road to find Bandit waiting for her in the usual spot. They reached the pumpkin-lined path of 13 Battington Lane a few minutes later. As they approached, the front door flew open with a wail like a banshee. (Have you ever heard a baby cry? Of course you have. It's a dreadful racket; imagine that but twice as loud.)

"Welcome home," said Helter-Skelter, stepping aside to allow them to pass. "Mummy says you're to change out of your uniform and come right back down. You'll be leaving for New York shortly."

"What about my after-school snack? There's a slice of pizza in the fridge…"

"There'll be plenty of time for pizza in New York. Off you go – pip pip!"

"There'd better be," Theodora grumbled, marching

up to her room where she quickly changed. She was just lacing up her trainers when Sherman appeared in a crack in the wall.

"Mummy said we're going to be late if we don't leave now," he said.

"I'm ready," Theodora replied, swinging her knapsack over her shoulder. "Weird, this feels heavier than it did a few minutes ago..."

"Why're you bringing your knapsack, anyway?"

"Because I've got *homework*, courtesy of Ms Frumple."

"Terrible," Sherman tsked.

"Tell me about it," she agreed, plucking him off the wall and placing him on her free shoulder. Two minutes later they arrived in the Hall of Reflection (a fantastical corridor made of mirrors). It was packed with monsters.

On one side were those who would be going to Manhattan, including: Mummy and Dracula, each holding a suitcase; Wilhelmina, clutching a carpetbag; and Grimeny Cricket, obsessively reviewing his itty-bitty flash cards (he would be presenting at the Monster United Nations in a few days' time; more on this shortly).

On the other side were the monsters who would *not* be going, including Helter-Skelter; Georgie and Bandit; Sir Pumpkin-de-Patch; Marty and the werewolf cubs; Bon; Gabe; Figaro; Pimms; the trolls; and the librarians: a skull named Hamlet and a raven named Mousetrap. Even Bob and Sally had left their perch on the roof to see them off. Only Goldie, the wosnak, was missing, but then she rarely left her tower (to the other monsters' relief, for she was notoriously powerful and rather bad-tempered: a deadly combination). But wait…

"Where's Sylvester? Theodora asked, suddenly noting the werewolf pup's absence.

"Good point," said Marty, scratching his whiskery chin as he mulled it over. "I haven't seen him in a while."

"I'll take a look," offered Helter-Skelter. "He probably got into the pantry again – I must remember to move the cub-treats to a higher shelf. Theodora, I hope you have a lovely holiday," he added, handing her an old-fashioned camera attached to a leather strap. "Your very first trip abroad!"

"Wow," Theodora breathed, placing the strap around her neck. "Thanks!"

"Eurga!" said Georgie, swooping down to give Theodora a hug.

"Meow!" Bandit seconded, bumping his head against her shins. Here, I suspect, he meant, "What Georgie said – we'll miss you!"

"We will," Bon nodded, ears flapping against his golden mane.

"Wish I could go," said Sir Pumpkin-de-Patch wistfully. "The Botanical Gardens are a sight to behold! But I don't dare leave my own garden at the moment – the weather-monster is calling for another frost."

"Youuuu must seeeee a perfooormance at the Metroooopolitan Operaaaa," sang Figaro.

"And make sure you eat at One if by Land, Two if by Sea," said Pimms. "My sister's been haunting it for years."

"We'll do all that and more," Dracula promised. "But now we really must be going."

Theodora gave each of the cubs a quick pat, then followed Dracula and Mummy to the other end of the corridor. Mummy slipped her hand into Theodora's. "Are you excited?"

"Yes!" Theodora crowed. "I can't believe we're going to America – and that I'm finally going to ride the *Glass Express*!"

"You'll be the first human ever to do so."

"Wow," she breathed.

"Now, pay close attention," Mummy said, releasing Theodora's hand and stepping towards the mirror. A dozen-odd reflections appeared in the glass.

"How can I help you?" asked one of the reflections.

"I ordered a transfer to the Manhattan MLM for 4 p.m.," the real Mummy said.

Mummy's reflection pulled a small clipboard from her wrappings. "Let's see," she said, flipping through the pages. "Yes, I've got it right here," she continued, swapping her clipboard for a conductor's hat, which she placed on her head. "The *Glass Express* is now boarding," she said, as the unmistakable sound of a train whistle shrieked in the distance. "All aboard!" She stepped aside, revealing an endless, empty space.

"Thanks," said Mummy, stepping forward and vanishing *into* the mirror.

"Whoa," said Theodora, as Wilhelmina also passed through the glass.

"Monster United Nations, here I come!" said Grimeny Cricket, hopping after them.

"You and Sherman go next, Theodora," said Dracula.

"OK," she agreed nervously; what would she find on the other side of the glass? This was another well-kept secret, and Theodora had no idea what to expect. It was called the *Glass Express*, but surely it wasn't an *actual* train? She'd never thought to ask. Well, she supposed there was only one way to find out: she straightened her hair ribbon, squared her shoulders, and stepped into the mirror. Moving through the glass was like taking a dip in a cool pond: a bit chilly, but not altogether unpleasant.

"Well, now we know what's on the other side of a mirror," Sherman mused as they passed through the glass.

"It's … not what I expected," Theodora whispered.

They had entered a large rectangular room. The walls were comprised of glass, the light (where was it coming from?) casting small, flickering rainbows across its surface. And there, on the other side of the room, was the Mummy reflection-cum-conductor.

"This way," she called, waving them over as the train whistle blew again. "Safe travels!" she said, urging them through a door Theodora hadn't noticed.

"Oh, my," breathed Sherman, taking in the sight before them.

And what a sight it was: they were standing in the well-heeled compartment of an old-fashioned train. It was lined with curtained booths and glossy tables, each of which held a bolted-on lamp and a scattering of menus. Grimeny Cricket had settled at – or rather, on – one of the tables, his notecards spread out before him. Mummy and Wilhelmina had taken seats in the booth on either side of him.

"Welcome!" called an unfamiliar voice.

Theodora's gaze travelled to the back of the compartment, where a bar made of gold glittered from floor to ceiling. Dozens of glistening bottles lined the shelves. A crocoman sporting an impressive handlebar moustache stood polishing a glass.

You are wondering, I am sure, what a crocoman is? A crocoman is a monster who resembles a crocodile

– if a crocodile stood upright and walked on two legs instead of four.

“What can I get for you?” he asked.

Theodora glanced at Mummy. “Is it OK if we order something?”

“It’s only half an hour to New York, so just get something small.”

“Wait, we’ll get to New York in *half an hour*? How does that work?”

“Magic,” Wilhelmina replied. “A team of warlock engineers built the *Glass Express* in nineteen twenty-two; it still runs on the force of their spells. The train connects the London MLM mansion to the Manhattan MLM penthouse, the Paris MLM chateau, the Cape Town MLM villa, and the Hong Kong MLM lodge all in under an hour. You should order now," she added.

Theodora and Sherman made their way up to the bar.

"I'm Miles," the crocoman said, introducing himself. "What can I get for you?"

"What do you have?"

Miles passed Theodora a menu, which read:

The Glass Express Bar,
offering the finest food and drink
for breakfast, lunch, tea and dinner

Theodora didn't know where to begin. The menu was several pages long and filled with foods she'd never heard of, like *Bouillabaisse* (a French seafood stew) and *Pad See Ew* (a Thai noddle dish).

"Might I suggest the tea?" offered Miles. "It's excellent."

"Tea sounds great," she said gratefully.

"Take a seat," he said, flashing a smile that was

a wee bit startling, given that his mouth was full of sharp, jagged teeth.

They returned to the booth, where Dracula had joined Mummy, Wilhelmina and Grimeny Cricket.

"Attention all passengers," said the conductor, appearing in the compartment. "The train is now departing." The whistle sounded once more as the conductor disappeared into the next compartment. A moment later the train began to move.

"Here you are," said Miles, placing two steaming mugs of tea and a tray of goodies – sandwiches and cakes, scones, clotted cream, and Sherman's

favourite: strawberry jam – in front of them. All of it was delicious, just as the barman had promised. And by the time they'd finished, the train slowed, then stopped altogether.

"The *Glass Express* has now arrived," came the conductor's voice over the loudspeaker. "The local time is 4.30 p.m. Please gather your belongings before exiting. Thank you for riding the *Glass Express*."

"How's it only 4.30 p.m.?" Sherman wondered. "Isn't New York five hours behind London?"

"All part of the train's magic," Wilhelmina said.

"Come," said Dracula, sliding out of the booth. "Boolivia's waiting for us."

Theodora scrambled out after him, asking, "Who's Boolivia?"

The Incidents

"Boolivia is Gabe's sister, and the mistress of the Manhattan MLM," Dracula explained. "We're staying at her invitation."

"Gabe never mentioned that he has a sister," Sherman said.

"A bit of sibling rivalry, I think," Grimeny Cricket supplied. "Boolivia is very successful; she graduated first in her class from Monstredame University and is one of the youngest ever agency heads – she's only one hundred and thirty-two!"

"And she's done wonders in reducing monster-crime across the city," Mummy added. "Her Reform School is one of the best in the country."

"When can we meet her?" Theodora asked eagerly.

Dracula smiled. "Soon." He led them off the train and into a glass room very like the one at the London

MLM mansion. On the other side of the mirror, however, was a room very *un*like any at the London MLM mansion: it was airy, spacious and modern. Everything was white, from the starburst light fixture to the leather sofas to the thick, plush carpet.

"Welcome to the Manhattan MLM," said a parrot-like voice.

The voice belonged to a bird – no, woman – no, bird-woman? Theodora wasn't sure; she'd never seen anything quite like her.

I, however, have seen *plenty* of bird-women in my day, and can confirm that the monster in question was in fact a harpy. Harpies have the head of a woman and the beak, wings, legs and tail of an oversized bird of prey. This particular harpy was dressed in a maid's uniform, complete with a doily on her head and a duster in her hand – er, talon.

"Are you Boolivia?" Theodora asked.

The harpy chuckled, the sound more like a bird's chirp than a human's laugh.

"Dear me, no. You'll know Boolivia when you see her. I'm Harriet. I manage the New York MLM household. And you must be Theodora," she said, dipping into a curtsy.

"How'd you know my name?"

"Inspector Shelley told us all about you. It seems you have quite a knack for getting into mischief," she added, eyes twinkling.

"Inspector Shelley?" Theodora cried, aghast. "She's not here, is she?"

"Dear me, no," Harriet chirped. "She was here for the Annual MLM Investigators' Conference, but she's gone now."

"Thank darkness," Wilhelmina said. "I wouldn't fancy running into her. Ever."

"Now, now," said Dracula. "Let's not be too – er, truthful. I mean, I'm sure it would be nice to see her again sometime – if not soon, then—"

"In four or five centuries, give or take," Wilhelmina supplied.

"Well... Quite," he finished sheepishly.

"It's lovely to see you again, Harriet," said Grimeny Cricket, covering the awkwardness of the moment.

"Grimeny Cricket!" she crowed, spotting him for the first time. "Dear me, we're so eager to hear your speech. It's all anyone can talk about!"

Perhaps this is a good time to remind you why we're in New York in the first place. Back in October, Grimeny Cricket published a brief regarding a spectacular bit of rule-breaking, which gained international attention, earning him an invitation to speak at the Monster United Nations in lower Manhattan, a great honour.

"Is it true that Headquarters committed a policy violation?" Harriet enquired.

"Allegedly," Grimeny Cricket corrected. "But between us, yes."

Harriet clucked her beak. "Shocking behaviour. Right, shall I take you to your rooms, or would you like to say hello to Boolivia first?"

"The latter, I think," Dracula replied.

"Leave your bags; the bellhop will bring them up."

Harriet led them down a portrait-lined corridor,

each depicting a famous monster, including Bone of Arc, a French warrior who'd led a skeletal army at the tender age of ninety-four and Werewolfgang Mozart, a Bavarian composer known for his stunning melodies. Doors appeared between the paintings, bearing plaques that read:

"The property has over three hundred rooms across forty-two floors," Harriet explained. "The lower levels are used for official MLM business, while the middle levels make up the Reform School. The upper floors house the hotel and permanent residences. Boolivia's quarters are at the very top."

Theodora's head was buzzing with all this information. And she couldn't even begin to imagine a building having *forty-two* floors! She found herself wishing she had about six more eyes (like Sherman) and four more ears to take it all in.

"I thought that speaker was excellent," she heard one witch say to another as they breezed past. "I'm going to buy her book."

"What's it called again?"

"*Lean In: Witches, Spellcasting, and the Will to Lead.*"

Harriet stopped at a row of elevator doors, where she flashed a skull-shaped badge at the attendant. They all piled into the elevator, which delivered them to the forty-second floor thirty seconds later. The doors opened directly into Boolivia's apartments, where they were greeted by a selkie secretary.

"Do you have an appointment?" asked the seal-like monster.

"Count Dracula for five o'clock," Harriet confirmed.

The selkie picked up the phone on her desk – a *human* ear with a dozen small gold hoops lining its ridge – and said, "Ms D'Ghoul, Count Dracula is here." She hung up the phone – er, ear. "Go on," she said, waving them into a large room across the corridor.

Sitting behind a desk groaning under piles of papers was a ghoul. Theodora knew at once that this was Boolivia; Harriet was right – she was impossible to miss. Like Gabe, everything about her was grey, from her skin to her eyes to her long, flowing hair – even her gown, an old-fashioned wedding dress complete with a veil, was the colour of slate. But while Gabe was rather quiet, preferring to keep to himself, Boolivia was vivacious and outgoing. Theodora liked her immediately.

"How lovely to see you all," she said warmly, coming round to greet her guests. Theodora thought she moved like a dancer; her feet barely seemed to touch the floor.

"And you. I'd like to introduce you to Sherman and Theodora," said Dracula, placing an icy hand upon Theodora's unoccupied shoulder.

"Charmed. Please, take a seat," Boolivia offered, leading them to a cluster of couches in the far corner. "How are things?"

"Not good. Not good at all, I'm afraid. We've had some distressing news," Dracula explained, proceeding to fill Boolivia in on Hilda's suspected reappearance and theft of the skele-crow.

As he spoke, Boolivia's eyes grew so wide and round that Theodora could see the whites – or, I should say, *greys* – of them on all sides. "But this is terrible!" Boolivia cried when he'd finished. "What if Hilda tries to take over Headquarters again?"

"We suspect that might be her eventual plan. We've alerted the proper authorities. I imagine you'll be receiving a letter from Headquarters soon."

"Perhaps Headquarters' post owl shall meet mine in flight..." she mused. "I've had to inform them of some – well, *incidents.*"

Mummy's brow furrowed. "Incidents?"

"Last week, I met with a witch who's lost the ability to cast spells. She'd tried a few remedial potions to no avail, so we signed her up for our Witch Empowerment series, thinking it was a confidence issue. When that didn't work, we sent her to a specialist. Nothing."

"Odd, indeed," Wilhelmina agreed.

"And over the weekend, a vampire staff member told us he no longer craves blood. He's been surviving on grape juice..."

Dracula shuddered. "Poor chap."

"And this all began recently?" Grimeny Cricket enquired.

Boolivia nodded. "Right around the time all this fog started rolling in... Not to mention the wind! And the temperature's dropped so low the pipes have frozen – a real nightmare for our spa facilities! I must admit, everyone is rather on edge."

"Curious, curious."

Theodora agreed: it *was* curious. Could it be a coincidence that these so-called incidents started right around the time that Hilda reappeared in Appleton? Somehow, she didn't think so. In fact, the more she thought about it, the more convinced she became that there was something in this theory... She would see what Sherman thought the next time they were alone.

And sure enough, Theodora would find what she was looking for; I daresay she might find *more* than she was looking for. Certainly, she would find more than she was bargaining for. Indeed, Theodora was about to stumble upon the most perilous – no, treacherous – no, deadliest – secret in all of monsterdom.

A secret which would change *everything.*

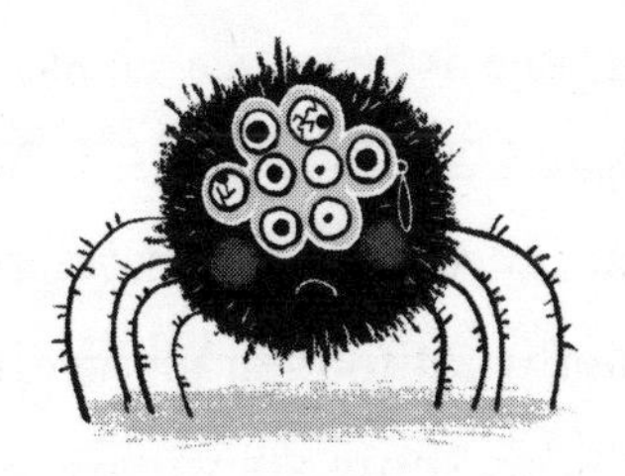

The Thickening of the Plot

This is probably a good time for a debrief. So far, we've learned that Hilda the hag has returned to Appleton and stolen her former monster-in-crime, the skele-crow, from the London MLM dungeons; the question remains, of course, as to *how* she accomplished this. We've also learned that a series of strange incidents have occurred at the New York MLM. And finally, we've learned that the horrible, holidays-hating Ms Frumple has given Theodora homework over the Christmas break.

Theodora, however, had no time to think about homework. There was simply too much to do, too much to see. That first evening alone offered much in the way of distraction: there was the fantastic feast that Harriet had prepared; the beautiful ballet performed by none other than Boolivia herself; and who could forget the appearance of a stowaway in Theodora's knapsack?

And the next day, when the Adebola family arrived – what's that? You want to hear about the stowaway? Fine; I suppose I can spare a few paragraphs.

After the feast on the first night, Theodora and Sherman said goodnight to the adults, then made their way to their room. Theodora flopped onto the bed, wondering if she could get away with sleeping in her clothes; she was very tired indeed. Sherman crawled down her arm, all eight of his eyes pinned upon the bulging bag sitting at the end of the mattress.

"Theodora, what's in your knapsack?" he asked.

"The usual," Theodora said, closing her eyes. "A granola bar, the new *Wilfred the Whimsical Warlock* comic, my homework. Why?"

"Well," Sherman said evenly, "it's moving."

Theodora's eyes popped open. "What do you mean, *it's moving*?"

The tarantula pointed a long, hairy leg at the bag.

Theodora gulped. He was right, it *was* moving. Summoning her courage, she unbuckled the front flap, flinging it open. And there, wriggling inside, was—

"*Sylvester!*" she cried, pulling the squirming cub

into her arms. "What are *you* doing here?"

Sylvester barked happily in reply.

"You naughty pup," she giggled as his slobbery tongue lapped against her cheek. "Did you sneak into my bag?"

"We should let Mummy know," said Sherman, looking relieved that nothing more terrifying than an errant werewolf cub had been hiding in the knapsack. "Marty must be worried sick."

Theodora sighed; so much for going straight to bed. "Let's go," she agreed, certain that Marty and Helter-Skelter must be frantically tearing the mansion apart in search of the pup.

And that is how Sylvester came to enjoy a holiday in the Big Pumpkin.

Now, as I was saying, early the next morning, Mummy, Theodora, Sherman and Sylvester met Dexter and his parents at Grand Central – incidentally, one of the most beautiful train stations in the world. (Trust me, I've seen them all.)

You're wondering how it's possible for a bunch of monsters to walk around New York City without catching anyone's notice – after all, wouldn't that be breaking ***Rule Number One:*** *Keep monsters hidden from humans*? You're right, of course, except for one teeny, tiny detail: the monsters were glamoured to look like people – at least, Mummy was, having taken the potion Wilhelmina had brewed for her that morning. (It was so successful that Mrs Adebola even complimented Mummy on her sweater.) Sherman and Sylvester hadn't taken any, but then the former was tucked safely out of sight inside Theodora's coat pocket while the latter was on the end of a lead out in the open, masquerading as a puppy.

Together, they piled into one of the city's famous yellow taxis. Unfortunately, this particular taxi reeked of garlic and stale cigarette smoke, a most unpleasant combination. They were very glad indeed when the ride was over. The cab dropped them off at Saks

Fifth Avenue, where they ogled the dazzling window displays. Then they went ice skating at Rockefeller Center, gliding beneath the rink's towering Christmas tree – well, Theodora did. I'm afraid Dexter spent more time on his backside than on his feet – as did Mr Adebola! At noon, they met a glamoured Wilhelmina and Dracula for lunch at One if by Land, Two if by Sea, a restaurant that was every bit as haunted as Pimms had said it was.

The next day was, if possible, even more exciting. They saw the Radio City Christmas Spectacular featuring the world-famous Rockettes, which Sherman especially enjoyed. They drank tea at the Plaza, which was the fanciest joint Theodora had ever been in. They visited the Statue of Liberty (which is actually a gargoyle; if I've said it once, I've said it a hundred times, monsters are *everywhere*). Dexter was especially excited to see this, rattling off a bunch of facts about its construction. And finally, the moment Theodora had been waiting for.

"I'm h-hungry," Dexter said as they left Central Park. It had just begun to snow, the soft, woolly flakes barely visible in the persistent blanket of fog Boolivia had told them about.

"Can we go for pizza?" Theodora asked hopefully.

"Well, I guess it's lunchtime," said Dexter's dad. "John's of Bleecker Street isn't too far from here." He turned to Mummy. "Shall we?"

Mummy agreed.

"Yes!" Dexter crowed, giving Theodora an excited thumbs-up. "It's the best!"

And to Theodora's delight, the pizza was every bit as good as Dexter had promised: a saucy, cheesy, crispy masterpiece of deliciousness. "This is the best pizza ever!" she declared through a mouthful of mozzarella.

And it must have been, for the restaurant's other patrons were exchanging similar sentiments … all except one.

Sitting in the very last booth was one person – no, *monster* (glamoured, of course) – who did not like the pizza at John's (or anywhere, for that matter). Nor did she like the humans crowding into the cramped, narrow space, and in fact she recoiled whenever one accidentally brushed against her. She certainly didn't like the red-headed child shovelling pizza into her mouth, and she absolutely *loathed* the dark-haired woman sitting beside her.

The monster had been trailing the group all over the city, waiting for the perfect moment to strike: the moment when she would finally – finally! – take her revenge upon the London MLM and the child they had so foolishly adopted.

But first, she had an appointment with one Boolivia D'Ghoul…

That night, Theodora and her family were going for dinner with Dexter's family. Dexter and his parents were staying with Mrs Adebola's sister, whom Dexter assured Theodora was an excellent cook. If Theodora was looking forward to it, Mummy was beside herself.

"I've never been to a dinner party hosted by humans before," she fretted, reapplying her lipstick for the third or fourth time.

"It'll be fine," said Theodora, who, having been ready for at least an hour, was sitting on the floor in Mummy's room performing a torat reading.

Unsurprisingly, the first card she drew was *The Lady.*

The second card she selected was *The Moon*. It featured a yellow crescent, an unsmiling face carved into its cratered surface. A pack of wolves stood beneath the moon sliver, howling into the night.

"Fear. Fright. Nightmares," said Sherman, peering at the card. "Not a good omen..."

"No," Theodora agreed, hoping this didn't mean that the dinner party would go badly. She threw down the last card, *The Future.*

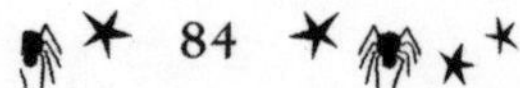

"The Empress again. Motherhood," Sherman murmured. "I wonder..."

"The car's here," called Wilhelmina, poking her head into the room.

"OK," said Theodora, shoving the torat cards into her pocket and dragging Mummy away from the dressing table.

"Make sure Sherman is well-hidden, Theodora," Wilhelmina said as they made their way downstairs. "New Yorkers don't take kindly to having large insects appear in their apartments. By the way, who's watching Sylvester?"

"Harriet. We didn't want to disturb Grimeny Cricket's preparations – his speech is tomorrow."

"Boolivia has graciously allowed us to use the MLM limo this evening," Dracula said as they approached, nodding at the shiny black car behind him.

They squeezed inside, chatting excitedly – all except for Dracula, who was unusually quiet. Every so often, he would glance at Mummy, open his mouth, then promptly close it. Finally, he cleared his throat and said, "Erm, Mummy?"

She turned expectantly.

"I – I..."

Mummy frowned. "Is everything all right?"

"Yes," he said, looking everywhere except at her. "I – youlookverynicethisevening," he said finally, the words tumbling out of his mouth in a jumble.

"Sorry? I didn't catch that."

Dracula took a breath. "I was just saying, you look very nice this evening."

Mummy lit up like the Christmas tree at Rockefeller Center. "Thank you! I'm wearing a new shade of lipstick, 'Vampire Ichor' by Monstree Lauder. Do you like it?"

"It's very pretty," he replied in a slightly strangled voice.

On the other side of the car, Wilhelmina looked stoic. Theodora had the distinct impression that she was trying not to roll her eyes, but couldn't figure out why.

"We're here," announced the chauffeur, interrupting Theodora's thoughts.

"Thank darkness," Wilhelmina muttered. "Theodora, are you sure Sherman is tucked away?"

"I'm going to miss so much in here," Sherman sighed from Theodora's pocket. "Make sure you all speak up so I can hear what's going on..."

They made their way over to the apartment block, a squat, six-storey building. They were buzzed in, then climbed up four flights of stairs, arriving outside a door marked 4B. Before they could knock, the door flew open to reveal Dexter's mum, smartly dressed in a skirt and matching gele wrapped elegantly around her head.

"Welcome," she said, ushering the guests inside with a wide grin. They hung their coats in the little foyer, then made their way into a large room. Theodora thought it looked more like a museum than a living room: paintings were crammed onto every available inch of wall while sculptures large and small dotted every available surface.

"Please, make yourselves comfortable," Mrs Adebola said with a smile.

"This place is so cool," Theodora said to Dexter, sitting beside him on the sofa.

Theodora and her family had just got settled when a stately woman entered the room, placing a platter of delicious-smelling food onto the coffee table. Like Mrs Adebola, she wore a gele, this one embroidered with silver thread. "I'm Dexter's aunt, Dede Idris," she said by way of introduction. "You must be Theodora."

"Nice to meet you. I like your gele," Theodora said, eyeing the shimmering fabric.

"I made it myself." Ms Idris grinned. "I own a textile business."

"Wow," Theodora said, suitably impressed.

"And this must be your family," Ms Idris continued, turning to Mummy. Her smile vanished as quickly as it had appeared. "You're..." she stammered. "You're..."

"Dede, what's wrong?" asked Dexter's mum, looking at her sister with concern.

Theodora glanced at Ms Idris, who'd gone all stiff and pale.

"They're ... they're..."

"Calm yourself," Mrs Adebola ordered. "Everything's fine."

"Everything's *not* fine," Ms Idris snarled. "Surely you can see – surely *you know what they are?*"

Mrs Adebola's eyes flashed in warning. "Would you excuse us?" she asked, an overly bright smile plastered onto her face. "Please, eat – the puff puff is delicious," she added as she dragged her sister out of the room. "And you must try the mosa!"

Theodora heard the click of a door, followed by the sound of muffled voices rising and falling. She shot Dexter a questioning look, but he just shrugged; he didn't seem to understand what was going on any more than she did.

"I'm sorry," said his dad, who clearly didn't either.

"I'm not sure what that's about..."

"Not at all," Mummy said lightly, flashing him a reassuring smile. But when he looked away, she exchanged a meaningful glance with Wilhelmina and Dracula.

"Please, eat," said Mr Adebola, beginning to hand out plates.

Dexter scooted forward, piling food high onto his plate. Theodora followed suit, and had just begun digging into her food when the sisters reappeared.

"Sorry about that," said Dexter's mum, sitting down beside Wilhelmina.

"Everything OK?" Mummy asked, nervously twisting a lock of hair around her finger.

"Yes. Right, Dede?"

"Right," her sister agreed stiffly.

Ms Idris didn't say much after that, though every so often Theodora caught her sneaking a glance at Mummy, or Wilhelmina, or Dracula with a shudder. Theodora didn't know what to make of her odd behaviour. (As for me, I have my suspicions...)

"What's on for tomorrow?" Mrs Adebola asked as they settled around the dining room table.

"We're going to the United Nations," Theodora said. "My uncle is giving a speech."

"Cool!" said Dexter, spearing a curried potato with his fork. "Can I come?"

"No!" cried Ms Idris, slamming her fork onto the table with such force that Theodora jumped. "Absolutely not!"

"*Dede!* What on earth has got into you?"

Ms Idris licked her lips. "I – I – I just thought Dexter and I could spend the day together... That's right." She nodded. "We could go to the New York Public Library. Or the movies. Or—"

"We can do all that on the weekend," Mrs Adebola interrupted. "We're here through New Year's Day; there's plenty of time. Of course Dexter can go," she told Mummy, as Dexter gave Theodora a high-five.

Ms Idris pursed her lips but said no more. In fact, she said no more the rest of the evening.

"That was weird," Dracula murmured at the end of the night, as they made their way back to the lobby.

"You don't think she knew—"

"This isn't the time to discuss it," Wilhelmina said tersely.

"This isn't the time to discuss what?" asked Theodora.

"Shh!"

But Theodora would not be deterred. "Ms Idris didn't seem to like us much, did she?"

The monsters exchanged another meaningful look but did not reply.

"What do you think she and Dexter's mum were arguing about?" Theodora tried again.

"That," Wilhelmina finally said, "is none of our business."

They did not speak during the journey back to the hotel, though this was not, Theodora sensed, because there was nothing to say; on the contrary, she had a feeling the monsters were just waiting until she and Sherman were out of earshot. Theodora felt very frustrated indeed (why do grown-ups keep so many secrets, anyway?) Little did she know that she was about to discover something that would put Ms Idris out of her mind entirely...

The Third Incident

The elevator opened onto the thirty-eighth floor of the MLM penthouse. Theodora and the monsters, uncharacteristically quiet, made their way to their rooms.

"Straight to bed," Mummy told Theodora and Sherman. "We've got to be up early and— Harriet, what's wrong?" she asked as the harpy, who appeared to be in great distress, approached.

Harriet's bottom lip trembled. "I-i-it's," she stammered, tears welling up in her great amber eyes. "Oh, Mummy, it's Boolivia!"

"What's happened?" Dracula asked at once.

"She didn't come down to supper, so I brought her a plate of food – poor thing works so hard, she forgets to eat," she managed between sobs. "And – and—"

"Where is she now?" Wilhelmina interrupted.

"H-her office..."

Wordlessly, Dracula, Mummy and Wilhelmina strode back to the elevators, Harriet flapping after them. Theodora glanced at Sherman, lifting an eyebrow in question.

He sighed. "Oh, go on."

Popping him onto her shoulder, Theodora raced after them, squeezing into the elevator just as the doors were closing. She was sure she was in for a talking-to, but no one even noticed she was there: Mummy was too busy consoling Harriet, and Dracula and Wilhelmina were already deep in a whispered discussion. When the doors reopened, they stumbled through the reception area and into Boolivia's office, where a cluster of monsters were gathered around the ghoul's desk.

"What's happened?" asked Mummy.

"We found her like this," Boolivia's assistant said in a shaking voice.

"Like *what?*"

The monsters stepped aside to reveal Boolivia, still sitting in her chair – except she didn't *look* like Boolivia. True, she was still grey and yes, she was still wearing a gown, but her expression was all wrong: her

gaze was vacant, as blank and unseeing as a corpse's. She was unnaturally still, her body stiff and wooden.

"What's wrong with her?" asked Sherman, aghast.

Mummy blinked at the sound of the tarantula's voice. Theodora was *sure* they'd be getting that telling off now, but Mummy only said, "I don't know."

"She looks like one of those puppets," Theodora said slowly, "the ones with the strings…"

"A marionette," Sherman supplied.

"Has she been seen by a doctor?" asked Wilhelmina.

A purple-skinned warlock with a long, white beard cleared his throat. "I've given her a preliminary examination. There's nothing wrong with her, as far as I can tell, other than…" He gestured vaguely.

"Harriet," said Dracula, "what did you do after you found Boolivia?"

The harpy opened her mouth to reply but was too overcome to speak.

"She found me," said the selkie, patting Harriet on the back. "I called security –" she jerked a thumb at a sasquatch – "and the doctor. Then I convened the New York MLM," she added, nodding at the cluster of monsters.

"Has there been any unusual activity in the hotel tonight?" Dracula asked the security sasquatch.

He shook his head.

"And has Boolivia had any unexpected visitors?"

"Not that I'm aware of," replied the selkie. "But I'm only on duty Mondays through Fridays from nine to five, and it's not unusual for Boolivia to take meetings out of hours."

"Can you please check her appointment book for today's schedule?"

"Right away," she agreed, scurrying out of the

office. She returned thirty seconds later, flipping through the diary. "Boolivia had an appointment at 8 p.m. tonight with one Thelda H. Gaih. There's no stated meeting purpose."

"Visitors have to register with Reception," put in the sasquatch. "They'd have taken additional details, a phone number and the like. I'll check."

"I need to place an urgent call," Dracula said, withdrawing a crumpled business card from his cape. A lopsided eye was scribbled on one side, the initials E.S.M.A. printed below it. With a jolt, Theodora realized she had

seen that card not once, but twice before…

"You can use my phone," offered the selkie, leading him into the reception area.

"We're going to transfer Boolivia to the hospital," the doctor told the room at large. "The ambulance will be arriving shortly."

Theodora shuddered at the thought. She'd only been to hospital once, to have her tonsils out, and she had been very nervous about the visit. Mummy and Dracula had stayed with her the whole time, and afterwards she'd been allowed to eat ice cream for dinner. But somehow, Theodora didn't think that Boolivia was going to be in for such a treat. She patted the ghoul's hand sympathetically, trying to avoid looking into her vacant eyes.

"We've called a meeting to discuss what's happened here," said a ghost with a mohawk. "We'd be grateful if you'd join us," she added.

"Certainly," Mummy agreed. "Harriet, can you please take Theodora and Sherman back to their room?"

Theodora opened her mouth to object but Mummy said, "There's nothing you can do for Boolivia now, Theodora. And we'll be of more use to the Manhattan MLM without having to worry about you, too."

“Maybe Sherman and I could go keep her company at the hospital…” Theodora suggested, keen to help.

“That’s a lovely idea,” Mummy said, giving Theodora’s shoulder a squeeze. “But I’m afraid in her current state Boolivia wouldn’t even notice that you were there.”

“How about when she wakes up—”

“Go,” Wilhelmina said, in a surprisingly stern, Mummyish voice. “Have a good, long rest. You’ll see; everything will look better tomorrow. It always does.”

Except, of course, when it doesn’t.

The following morning, Mummy, Wilhelmina, Theodora, Sherman and Sylvester (wearing a cheerful red leash and matching collar) arrived outside Ms Idris’s apartment at 9 a.m. sharp to collect Dexter. Dracula had stayed behind to assist the NY MLM in Boolivia’s absence, and Grimeny Cricket was already at the Monster United Nations. Dexter’s parents came out to say hello, but Ms Idris did not join them. Theodora thought she saw the curtain fluttering in the fourth-floor window and wondered if Dexter’s aunt was watching them, and why she seemed to have taken such a dislike to her family.

"Grimeny Cricket must b-be so excited," Dexter said as they got into the cab.

"He is." Wilhelmina smiled. "The Monster UN is typically closed at this point in the year, but Gorgana, the Head of the General Assembly, has called a special session for Grimeny Cricket to share his report."

"Must b-be some r-report."

"Indeed. Why, they've even granted special permission for you and Theodora to attend. That doesn't happen every day!"

The cab arrived at the Monster UN twenty minutes later. The UN building – a dark, gothic structure built in the mid-1800s – was impossible to miss, clocking in at a whopping fifty storeys. It was so tall that the roof's many turrets weren't even visible, obscured by swirling grey clouds and stagnant swatches of the ever-persistent low-hanging fog. One by one, Theodora, Dexter and the monsters pushed through the revolving doors, stepping into a marble-pink lobby.

"Name?" asked a bored-looking monster glamoured to look like a security guard.

Mummy gave him their names.

"Go in," he said, handing them each a badge.

As they walked through the turnstiles, Mummy and Wilhelmina shrugged off their glamours with sighs of relief, then rounded the corner to find themselves in a corridor packed with monsters. The attendees shuffled into the General Assembly room, a vast, circular chamber. Narrow windows dotted the stone walls, allowing slits of light to slant into the room. Benches rose towards the ceiling, stadium-style. Mummy led them over to a section marked: RESERVED, LONDON MLM.

"There's Grimeny Cricket!" said Sherman excitedly. They all waved at the bug, who was sitting with the other speakers in the front row, then took their seats. When the chamber had reached capacity, Gorgana, a gorgon (a woman with real, live snakes for hair), approached the podium. She tapped a claw-like hand against the microphone.

"Welcome to the eight-hundredth meeting of the Monster United Nations General Assembly," she began. "Today's agenda is as follows: we'll take attendance, then review the Dubai MLM's update on the glamour potion shortage in the Middle East. We'll hear a report on rising sea levels from the Loch Ness

Monster, who's dialling in from Scotland. Our keynote speaker is Grimeny Cricket, who'll be sharing a brief regarding an alleged breach of protocol made by Headquarters. We'll conclude by opening the floor to any other business."

After attendance was taken, each speaker took his or her place at the podium. It seemed to Theodora that each one droned on longer than the last. Unsurprisingly, her attention soon began to wander. She glanced around the room, finding the monsters infinitely more interesting than the speeches. Her gaze flicked up to the ceiling, where the rafters were full of birds: swarms of sparrows, passels of pigeons and a lone crow.

Finally, it was Grimeny Cricket's turn. The bug hopped onto the podium, carefully spreading out his notes. Theodora pulled her attention back to the front of the room. Gorgana adjusted the microphone for him, lowering it to a cricket-friendly height. Looking very nervous indeed, Grimeny Cricket straightened his cloak, then began his speech. A speech that, I'm afraid, he would not have the chance to finish.

The Monster United Nations

"Honourable members of the General Assembly," Grimeny Cricket began, "I thank you for allowing me to present my brief, 'The International Code of Monster Relations: Governmental Responsibilities', inspired by a recent situation that arose between Headquarters and the London MLM.

"As you may be aware, ten years ago the members of the London MLM – myself included – adopted one Theodora Hendrix, a human child."

This declaration was met by an outcry of mutterings; it seemed that many of the monsters were not, in fact, aware.

"Did he just say they adopted a *human* child?" sputtered a nymph with long, golden strands of wheat growing out of her skull.

"Nah," replied her ogre companion. "Illegal, ain't it?"

"But look! Just a few rows down. That's a girl-child," the nymph said in a carrying whisper, pointing in Theodora's direction. "Do you think it's *her*?"

Theodora quickly looked down, but the surrounding monsters had overheard the nymph's words; soon they were all craning their necks to get a look at Theodora, whose face was now burning. Dexter seemed to shrink beside her, as if he were trying to make himself less noticeable too.

"Order!" cried Gorgana, banging a gavel on the head table.

The chatter subsided, replaced by a thorny silence.

Rattled by the audience's response, Grimeny Cricket cleared his throat before ploughing on. "We knew that in adopting Theodora we were breaking ***Rule Number One***. However, we also knew that in breaking the first rule we were upholding the second.

Theodora was discovered in a hobgoblin-infested graveyard, and had we failed to act she would have surely been eaten. Our search for her parents was unsuccessful, as were our attempts to place her with our human neighbours. And so, Theodora became ours."

As Grimeny Cricket spoke, Theodora felt a sudden pain in her hip, as if she'd received a sharp, hot jab. "Ouch," she muttered, hand flying to her side.

"What's wrong?" asked Sherman.

"Not sure..."

The heat seemed to be coming from her skirt pocket, where she'd put her torat pack for safe keeping. She slipped a hand inside, surreptitiously withdrawing the deck and flipping through the cards. Theodora wasn't sure exactly what she was looking for, but figured she would know it when she saw it.

"Headquarters found us Not Guilty of any wrongdoing," Grimeny Cricket continued. "However, they sent an inspector to confirm there was no additional rule-breaking. Two weeks into the inspector's stay, Headquarters indicated that Theodora might remain with the London MLM permanently."

Only half-listening, Theodora continued thumbing through the deck, pausing when she reached *The Lady*.

"Theodora," Sherman whispered urgently, "do you see—"

"Shh," Dexter hushed them. "You're m-missing Grimeny Cricket's speech."

Theodora didn't reply; she was staring at the startling – no, stunning – no, shocking – sight that was *The Lady* card: the golden-haired woman was *moving*, straightening her robes and shaking out her mane of hair as if she'd just awoken from a long nap.

"But per the UK Code of Monster Relations, Monster Parliament obliges Headquarters to present any new requirements – including staffing arrangements – to Number Ten Drowning Street before changes are made. However, Headquarters bypassed these, setting a dangerous precedent for—"

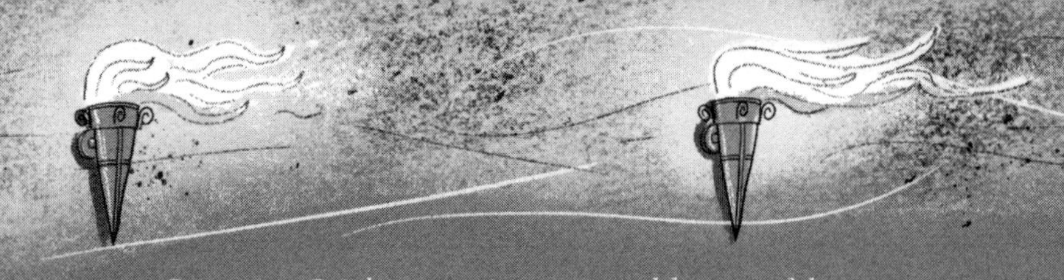

Grimeny Cricket was interrupted by a sudden, thunder-like clap. At the same time, all the lights winked out, leaving only a smattering of torches flickering throughout the chamber. A gust of wind – where was it coming from? – whooshed around the auditorium, rustling the assembled monsters' hair and fur and feathers.

Sylvester whimpered, squirming on Theodora's lap.

"Mummy," Theodora whispered, the torat cards all but forgotten, "what's happening?"

"Something's wrong," Wilhelmina said before Mummy could reply.

As if in agreement, a terrible laughter echoed throughout the room. "Ah, the Monster UN," croaked a voice over the loudspeaker. Theodora shuddered – there was something horribly familiar about that voice. "It's been so long since I've seen this most un-hallowed place."

Mummy and Wilhelmina exchanged a startled look.

"You don't think…?" Mummy began.

"It's possible," Wilhelmina said.

"And how lovely to see so many familiar faces

joined in that most *noble* pursuit of upholding the MLM Charter. But did you know," the speaker said, voice dropping conspiratorially, "that there are those amongst you who do *not* support the Charter? Those who wish, as I do, for it to be torn up and thrown out?"

Was it just Theodora's imagination, or had the temperature dropped? What had started as a gentle breeze was now a raging windstorm, stinging her eyes and pushing loose strands of hair into her mouth. The blustery squalls tore through the auditorium, snuffing out the torches and ripping them off the walls. Darkness descended upon the chamber, the narrow windows providing the only meagre source of light.

"I d-don't like this," Dexter stammered.

"Woof!" Sylvester agreed.

Theodora, distracted by a flickering out of the corner of her eye, didn't reply. Was it just a trick of the light, or was something there, hidden amongst the shadows?

"Mummy," she said, pulling at her wrappings. "What are those?"

"What are what?"

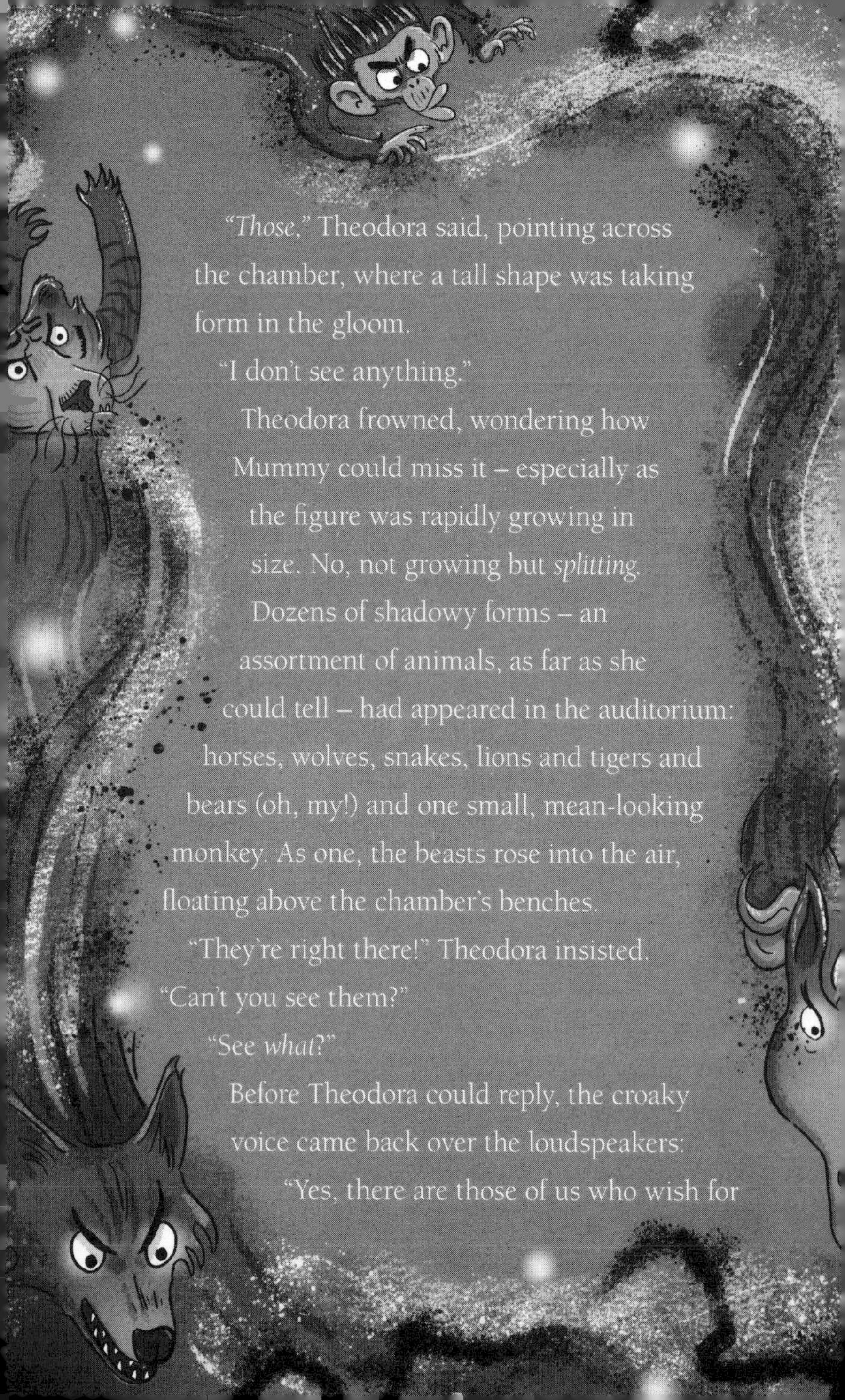

"Those," Theodora said, pointing across the chamber, where a tall shape was taking form in the gloom.

"I don't see anything."

Theodora frowned, wondering how Mummy could miss it – especially as the figure was rapidly growing in size. No, not growing but *splitting*. Dozens of shadowy forms – an assortment of animals, as far as she could tell – had appeared in the auditorium: horses, wolves, snakes, lions and tigers and bears (oh, my!) and one small, mean-looking monkey. As one, the beasts rose into the air, floating above the chamber's benches.

"They're right there!" Theodora insisted. "Can't you see them?"

"See *what*?"

Before Theodora could reply, the croaky voice came back over the loudspeakers:

"Yes, there are those of us who wish for

monsters to take our rightful place,
ruling over humans as we once did. As we were meant to do! Join us as we return to our former glory! But stand in our way, and I give you fair warning: you shall pay the price..."

"Who *are* you?" demanded Gorgana. "Show yourself!"

"As you wish..."

Another thunder-like clap reverberated throughout the chamber. As if on cue, the crow perching on the rafters took flight, circling the room in search of something – or perhaps some*one*. Having spotted his quarry, he plummeted towards the ground, soaring through the slivers of light seeping in from the windows. As he did, his feathers vanished, as did the carroty irises of his eyes and the scaly skin of his feet. A skeleton emerged in his place.

You're right, of course, it was a skele-crow – the very skele-crow who had escaped from the MLM dungeons. Gliding back into the shadows, the fowl returned to its fleshy form, landing neatly atop a walking stick.

A walking stick that belonged to...

The Shadowmongers

"Hilda!" Wilhelmina spat.

The intruder threw back her hood, revealing a clever, weathered face with beetle-black eyes. "At your service," the hag said, bowing mockingly.

“Shadowmongers?” Gorgana repeated, a note of fear creeping into her voice. “Impossible. They were banished to Antarctica upon the signing of the MLM Charter some three thousand years ago!”

“Well,” Hilda said baldly, “I’ve un-banished them.”

“Even you, Hilda, would not align yourself with such evil creatures!”

“I’m afraid you’ve underestimated me, my dear Gorgana.”

“Are th-they here n-now?” stammered the wheat-haired nymph, glancing frantically around the room.

“Oh, yes,” Hilda breathed, a wicked gleam sliding into her eyes. “Very much so.”

Upon hearing these words, the nymph made a run for it, flinging herself against the chamber doors only to find that they were locked. And she wasn’t the only one hoping to escape; within seconds a dozen or so monsters had joined her, desperately banging against the exit doors. A shiver ran down Theodora’s spine as she watched the scene unfold. What sort of monster was bad enough to scare other monsters this badly?

"Surrender!" Hilda bellowed. "Or find yourselves caught in the Shadowmongers' snare!"

"Never!" Gorgana yelled to a smattering of cheers.

"Have it your way," Hilda hissed. "Shadowmongers, ATTACK!"

At this, the beasts swarmed, their hooves and paws and feet pounding against the air as easily as they would the earth. One by one, they broke free of the pack, targeting the monsters below. A shadowy horse was the first to strike, galloping towards the nymph. Theodora watched, mesmerized, as the creature went – there was no other word for it – *through* her. The nymph let out a blood-curdling scream; the golden strands had fallen out of her head, forming a pile at her feet.

Another scream tore through the air as a lion charged through a young rata-tat-tat. Her skin immediately shrivelled and creased, wrinkling as if she'd aged sixty years. At the same time, a bear swiped its paw through a ghost, who vanished on the spot. And then Theodora saw something that made her blood run cold: the monkey, heading straight for the podium where Grimeny Cricket…

"Grimeny Cricket!" she shrieked, sending Sylvester

tumbling to the floor as she jumped to her feet. "Look out!" But it was too late; the monkey had soared through the cricket.

Horror-struck, Theodora stumbled out of the row, flying down the steps and skidding to a stop beside the podium. "Grimeny Cricket, are you OK?" she asked, rising to her tiptoes, the better to see him.

But the cricket did not reply. Instead, he hopped off the podium and across the room.

"CATCH THAT CRICKET!" Theodora cried,

terrified that in all the chaos her friend would be squashed like a – well, a bug. Dexter gave chase, trying – and failing – to catch the cricket in his cupped hands.

"Pimpken-Frimpkin, rubbedly-coo!" Wilhelmina shouted, waving her wand. A small, gilded cage appeared out of thin air, trapping the cricket. Dexter made a grab for it.

"Theodora," Mummy gasped, appearing at her side and pulling her into a hug. "Don't run off like that!"

Theodora was surprised to see that Mummy's hands were shaking. Her stomach lurched as if she'd missed a step; it was one thing for the other monsters to be frightened, but quite another for Mummy to be.

"What's *happened* to him?" Mummy asked

as Wilhelmina, Sylvester and Dexter, still holding the cage, joined them.

"What's happened to half the room?" Wilhelmina retorted with a wave of her hand.

"It's those *things*," Theodora said. "Those Shadowmongers. The monkey flew through Grimeny Cricket, and—"

"We've got to get out of here," Sherman interrupted.

"—then he hopped off the podium," she continued. "I yelled at him to stop, but—"

"How? The d-doors are locked," Dexter replied to Sherman.

"—he didn't seem to hear me," Theodora finished.

"I'll take care of that," Wilhelmina told Dexter, rolling back her sleeves. "Witches!" she yelled, raising her voice above the din. "Your strongest lock-breaking spell on my count. Three, two, one…"

A dozen wands rose into the air. *"Rallabay, Rallabee!"* the witches shouted.

The great doors popped open with a click. The

monsters who'd gathered at the exit heaved them open, hastening out the chamber. Seeing this, Hilda raised her staff to stop them. A group of trolls rushed at her, but the hag was too quick for them. She banged her walking stick against the floor, dislodging the skele-crow from his perch. A dazzling light exploded from its tip, hitting the fowl square in the middle of his feathery chest. He let out a squawk of surprise. And then his beak was extending, his wings expanding, his head enlarging. The skele-crow was now almost the size of a pony.

"Come, my pretty!" Hilda called.

Dutifully, the engorged skele-crow soared towards the hag, landing smoothly beside her. He fell to his scaly knees, allowing Hilda to scramble onto his back, then took off. Another jet of light burst forth from Hilda's walking stick, blasting a hole into the nearest wall. And before the smoke had even cleared, they had disappeared through it.

"We've got to stop her," said Mummy, moving towards the still-smoking hole.

"No!" Wilhelmina cried. "You're forgetting the Shadowmongers. Who knows where they've gone? We could be walking into a trap!"

“They’re still here,” Theodora confirmed, watching as one of the wolves sprinted towards a vampire.

Mummy’s eyes widened. “You can see them?”

Theodora threw up her hands. “That’s what I’ve been trying to tell you!”

“Lucky for us,” said Wilhelmina, shooting her a quick smile before taking the cage from Dexter and carefully tucking it inside her cape. “Keep your eyes open, Theodora,” she said seriously, urging them towards the exit.

They joined the queue of monsters shuffling out of the chamber, and soon reached the lobby, which, as you can imagine, was in a state of disarray: monsters were jostling one another, shouting and fighting in their haste to escape through the revolving doors.

"This way," said Wilhelmina, dragging Theodora and Dexter off to one side, away from the worst of it.

"Where's Mummy?" Theodora asked, noticing that she was no longer behind her.

Dexter glanced around the lobby. "T-there," he said, pointing to the other side of the room, where Mummy was huddled with a half-dozen monsters, whom Theodora recognized as the MLM agency heads.

"Never mind Mummy," said Wilhelmina, dropping to a knee so that she was eye-level with the children. "I want you to pay close attention to what I'm about to say. It could be a matter of life or death. Do you understand?"

Theodora did not understand but did not dare to say so. She had never seen Wilhelmina looking so intense; she could practically feel the anxiety roiling off the witch in waves.

"No matter what happens, don't tell anyone that you can see the Shadowmongers. And take this," Wilhelmina said, pushing a small, surprisingly heavy, pouch into her hands.

Theodora turned it over to find three rather ominous words stitched into the leather:

Emergency Use Only

"If something happens to me or Mummy…" Wilhelmina began.

"What—?"

"Do not interrupt! If something happens to me or Mummy, or if we become separated, I want you to open this pouch. You have my express permission to use whatever's inside it to protect yourselves," she said, levelling a severe look at Theodora, Dexter, Sherman and an unusually quiet werewolf pup. "But you are not to open it otherwise. *Understand?*"

Before Theodora could reply, a series of shouts erupted; the Shadowmongers had entered the lobby, striking down monsters left and right.

"The Shadowmongers!" Theodora cried. "They're here!"

"Let's go," Wilhelmina said, pushing through the crowd.

"One is headed this way," Theodora warned, as the mean-looking monkey who'd struck down Grimeny Cricket leapt towards them.

"It's t-too crowded," Dexter stammered. "We'll n-never make it."

"Oh, yes, you will," said Wilhelmina, slashing her wand through the air like a sword, Theodora felt something whoosh over her head, followed by the strangest of sensations: it was as if an invisible hand was pressing against the small of her back, pushing her forward. And then she, Dexter, Sherman and Sylvester were all moving towards the doors with ease, their paths magically cleared. But Wilhelmina's act of selflessness came at a price: in the brief time it took her to cast the spell, the Shadowmonger had closed the distance between them.

Theodora looked back just in time to see the monkey strike Wilhelmina. The witch stumbled back, wand tumbling out of her hand and rolling across the floor. Theodora tried to turn back to help but found that her legs would not obey, compelled onward by the witch's last spell. She craned her neck but couldn't see what was happening… And the next thing she knew, Theodora was being pulled through the revolving doors and deposited into the street.

Puppy Power

The children found themselves standing in the middle of the pavement, surrounded by fleeing monsters. Theodora wondered if the humans striding down said pavement would spot said monsters (most of whom weren't glamoured), but no one seemed to notice. (Which honestly isn't all that surprising; it *is* New York, after all.) But never mind *that* – she had to get back inside the Monster UN building where Wilhelmina was – well, Theodora didn't know, exactly. And what had happened to Mummy?

And then Theodora saw something that made her heart skip a beat: the Shadowmongers, pouring out of the revolving doors and into the winter-white sky like black, billowing plumes of smoke.

"The Shadowmongers," Theodora whispered. "They're here!"

Dexter's head whipped around. "W-where?"

"Does it matter?" she cried, stamping her foot in exasperation. "You can't see them!"

"We need to get out of here. Now!" Sherman said from her shoulder. "Shadowmongers are every bit as dangerous to humans as they are to monsters."

Curious, Theodora opened her mouth to ask what he meant by this, but one look at the tarantula's face and she promptly closed it; clearly, this wasn't the time for questions. Clutching Sylvester's leash tightly in her fist, she took off down the road, running as fast as her legs could carry her.

"How rude!" cried a lady in a long fur coat as Sylvester streaked past, nearly knocking her over.

"Sorry!" Theodora called over her shoulder, barely managing to hang on to his leash.

Some minutes later, Dexter gasped, "I c-can't k-keep running."

"We should find a place to regroup," Sherman agreed from Theodora's shoulder.

"This way!" Theodora said, indicating a deserted, graffiti-covered alley. They ducked behind an oversized refuse bin, noses wrinkling at the rancid smell. (They're lucky it wasn't summertime; there is

nothing – and I mean nothing – worse than the smell of rubbish rotting beneath the blazing August sun.) Seemingly unbothered by the odour, Sylvester dived head-first into a bin, happily wading through the mess.

"What are those things – those S-Shadow-m-mongers?" Dexter gasped, clutching at a stitch in his side.

Sherman cleared his throat. "Born of the shadows, Shadowmongers are among the vilest creatures to ever roam the earth. Invisible to the monster and human eye – well, most human eyes –" he amended, his gaze flicking to Theodora, "they use this gift of invisibility to set a trap, ensnaring those poor souls unfortunate enough to stumble across their paths. A monster struck by a Shadowmonger will lose its powers – whatever it is that makes them a monster, so to speak."

"L-like turning a highly intelligent cricket into a garden insect?"

"Or like turning a ghoul into a marionette," said Theodora, picturing Boolivia as she had last seen her: a life-sized wooden doll. "Sherman, how do you know all this?"

The tarantula shrugged. "Read it somewhere, I suppose – well, I need something to do while you're in school all day."

"W-what do Shadowmongers d-do to humans?"

"Their effect is more muted, though still rather horrifying: a human struck by a Shadowmonger will never know another night's rest, for their dreams will become nightmares forevermore."

"You mean – what *do* you mean?" Theodora frowned.

"A human struck by a Shadowmonger will have nightmares every single night for the rest of their life."

Dexter shuddered. "That's t-terrible."

"Quite," agreed Sherman. "Many have been driven mad by it – which is why we need to get out of here and back to the MLM. Anyone have any money?"

"I've g-got ten bucks," Dexter said, digging around in his pocket, "but that won't b-be enough to get us d-downtown."

"Theodora?" Sherman prompted.

But she wasn't paying attention; two Shadowmongers – a pair of lions – had glided into the alley, eyes shining like Christmas baubles. Theodora's eyes widened in fear, heart thumping against her ribcage, hands shaking at her sides.

"Shadow-m-mongers?" asked Dexter, watching her closely.

"Yes," she said, jerking her head towards the approaching creatures.

"This might be a good time to open Wilhelmina's

pouch," suggested Sherman.

In reply, Theodora passed Sylvester's leash to Dexter and withdrew the pouch from her pocket. She pulled apart the drawstrings, tipping the contents of the bag into her hand. An odd assortment of items tumbled out: there was the Sight Extender, an instrument used to destroy curses, which resembled a magnifying glass (except for the bright blue eyeball encased inside it) and which usually resided in the Ancient Curse Breaking Room at home; a colourful handkerchief embroidered with the initials "DI"; and a photograph featuring Theodora opening her presents last Christmas, surrounded by the smiling members of the London MLM.

"Maybe the Sight Extender can destroy Shadowmongers?" Sherman mused. "It worked on those evil mummies at Halloween..."

Figuring it was worth a try, Theodora aimed the instrument at the lions who were slinking down the alley, their molten eyes pinned upon her. She held her breath, hoping the eyeball would blink, that the white-bright light would burst forth from its lens as it had the last time she'd used it, but nothing happened.

"It's not w-working," Dexter said.

"Thank you, Captain Obvious," Theodora snapped.

"What should we do?" Sherman moaned, his pincers clicking anxiously.

"I'm thinking," Theodora replied, forcing herself to remain calm as the lions floated nearer and nearer still.

Now, I don't know about you, but if two creatures

who had the ability to make monsters lose their powers and humans have eternal nightmares were looming over *my* head, I certainly wouldn't remain calm: I would shriek like a banshee, jump into the dustbin along with Sylvester, and hope that the Shadowmongers had an aversion to rubbish.

But Theodora was not prone to shrieking, did not fancy diving into a dumpster, and did not think it likely that the Shadowmongers would be deterred by the rubbish even if she did. Instead, she returned the items to the pouch, tucking it inside one pocket. She shoved her hand inside her other pocket, a plan taking shape in her mind. Dexter wasn't going to like it – but then, he probably wouldn't like being attacked by a Shadowmonger, either.

"Got 'em," she muttered, withdrawing two long, grey feathers from her coat. And not just any feathers: Anca feathers. Never one to pass up the opportunity to be around anything monstrously magical – or perhaps I should say, magically monstrous? – Theodora had nicked a few feathers from the dungeons the day they had discovered the skele-crow's absence, thinking it might be fun to fly around the hotel corridors if things got a bit dull.

"Here," she said, passing one of the feathers to Dexter.

"What's this f-for?"

"To get us out of here," Theodora said impatiently. "Sylvester, come!"

To her surprise – and immense relief – the pup popped his head out of the bin, snout still buried in a Chinese take-away carton, and Dexter quickly hefted the smelly cub into his arms.

"Hold it up like this," Theodora said, demonstrating with her own feather. "When I give the signal, say 'Up'."

"What's the s-signal?"

"UP!"

"Up!" Dexter repeated, and just in time: the lions swooped, pouncing onto the very spot he'd been standing mere seconds earlier. But the beasts were too late.

Theodora felt her feet lifting off the concrete, and heard Dexter's yelp as his followed suit. Then they were flying, zooming *up* the side of the skyscraper, superhero-style. And though it felt as if she'd left her stomach somewhere back in the alley, Theodora's spirits soared. She was flying faster than a bird – no,

plane – no, rocket! The Shadowmongers would never catch them now; those beasts could fly, but not like *this*… They had escaped!

Dexter, however, did not share her exhilaration: he looked positively green and was, to put it bluntly, screaming his head off.

Within seconds they had reached the top of the building. They hovered in mid-air for a moment, then crashed into the roof tiles in a jumble of limbs and leash.

"Don't squish me!" exclaimed Sherman, scuttling out of reach.

"Sorry," Theodora said, rubbing her elbow. "Dexter, are you OK?"

This was a rather silly question. Dexter was clearly *not* OK, given that he was being rather violently ill over the side of the roof.

"There, there," said Sherman kindly, crawling up Dexter's arm and patting him on the shoulder.

"At least we g-got away from the Shadow-m-mongers," said Dexter, lifting his head and wiping the back of his hand across his mouth.

"No," Theodora said, her heart sinking like a brick dropped into a well. "We *didn't*."

And she was right: though they could not fly as fast as the children, the Shadowmongers could still fly, and they were now less than five metres away, drifting almost lazily up the side of the building.

Theodora scrambled to her feet, roughly pulling both Dexter and Sylvester away from the edge. They scurried across the rooftop, throwing themselves against a door she hoped would let them into the building. It was locked – of course it was. A heavy chain was padlocked around the handles.

"What are we going to do?" Sherman wailed.

The Shadowmongers, still visible only to Theodora,

were now close enough that she could see the strings of drool dripping from their fangs. Instinctively, she reached for Dexter's hand. "Your aunt was right," she whispered. "You shouldn't have come. I'm so sorry..."

"At l-least we're t-together," her friend replied, squeezing her hand in return.

Down by Theodora's ankles, Sylvester let out a howl, and, with a determined snarl, he reared onto

his back legs, frantically pushing his snout between Theodora's and Dexter's hands.

"He's t-trying to get at t-the door," Dexter observed, moving to the side.

"No," Sherman said shrewdly. "He's trying to get at the lock!"

And so he was: the werewolf cub, who moments before had seemed positively puppyish, now looked fiercely wolfish. He was snarling, ears flat against his head, as his sharp, strong teeth gnashed against the links of the chain again and again.

"Whatever he's trying to do, he'd better do it quick!" Theodora cried.

And then two things happened at once: the chain broke with a screech just as the lions pounced. Moving faster than Theodora had ever seen him move, Dexter pulled away the remains of the padlock and heaved the door open. He, along with Sherman and Sylvester, made it across the threshold just as the Shadowmongers struck.

Theodora, however, did not.

The Secret Life of Mrs Adebola

The lions soared right through Theodora's chest, one after the other. Her vision went black, filled with the smoke of the Shadowmongers' churning forms, as an arctic cold washed over her. Just as suddenly her vision cleared, though the chilled feeling remained (and would, I fear, for quite some time). Blinking rapidly as her eyes adjusted to the pale winter light, Theodora could just make out the two Shadowmongers, prowling towards the stairs upon which Dexter, Sherman and Sylvester stood, waiting for her.

"Run!" Theodora screamed, racing towards the stairs, hair streaming behind her like a cape. "They're here!"

They didn't need telling twice; Dexter and Sylvester moved as one, running down staircase after staircase. (I must take a moment to remind you that you should never run up or down the stairs as it's quite dangerous, but I'm sure you'll agree that in this case an exception had to be made.) A few minutes later they reached the ground floor, flinging open a (thankfully unlocked) door and spilling into an alleyway.

"That w-was close," Dexter panted, slamming the door shut behind them. "They almost g-got us."

"Almost," Theodora said, avoiding his gaze. Of course, the Shadowmongers hadn't *almost* got her – they *had* got her. According to Sherman, a lifetime of nightmares awaited her. Theodora bit her lip, pushing the thought from her mind. No point thinking about that now, she told herself firmly.

"We were very lucky indeed," Sherman agreed, jumping from Dexter's shoulder to Theodora's. "Now, let's quit while we're ahead. Does anybody know how to get back to the Manhattan MLM from here?"

The children shook their heads.

"What about your aunt's, Dexter?"

"I d-don't know how to g-get to Aunt Dede's apartment from here," he said apologetically. Then a thoughtful expression flickered across his face. "Wait…"

"What is it?"

"Theodora, c-can I have that pouch Wilhelmina g-gave you?" Dexter said. "I've just had a thought."

Theodora handed it to him. Dexter quickly pulled it open and withdrew the brightly coloured handkerchief, turning it over in his hands. "Aha!" he said excitedly. "I thought this looked familiar! See the initials, 'DI'? Dede Idris!"

"So?"

"So, Wilhelmina's a genius," Dexter said, dropping into a crouch beside Sylvester. "Here, boy." He held the cloth out to the cub, who sniffed it. "Can you follow the scent?"

"Woof!"

And so he could. As you may or may not know, werewolves have an excellent sense of smell. Oh, yes – their snouts are very powerful indeed, able to pick up a scent from a single object and trace it all the way back to the person, monster or animal to which it originally belonged. Sylvester was no exception.

Having caught Ms Idris's scent on the handkerchief, he followed his nose out of the alley and down the pavement. Half an hour later they found themselves standing outside Ms Idris's block. Dexter let them up to his aunt's apartment.

The four of them traipsed into the living room, where Dexter's aunt was sitting on the sofa drinking a cup of tea. She jumped at the unexpected sight of the children, sending the teacup flying. "You gave me a fright," she said, hand fluttering to her chest.

"Is everything OK?" Dexter's mum called from the next room.

"Dexter's here," Ms Idris shouted back.

"He's back early!" Mrs Adebola replied, striding into the room. "Dexter, you're here! You're *filthy*. And what," she asked, wrinkling her nose, "is that smell?"

"Rubbish," Theodora said helpfully.

"Hi, Theodora. But where are your parents?"

"Erm, they're – well..."

Dexter's aunt came to her rescue – sort of. "Do you see this?" she hissed, glaring first at Sherman, perched on Theodora's shoulder, and then at Sylvester, who was rolling around on the formerly pristine rug. "She's brought more of *them* into my house! And I'll take that, thank you!" she snapped, grabbing the drool-soaked handkerchief out of Sylvester's jaws.

Theodora's eyes narrowed. "What do you mean by 'them'?"

"She just means your pets," Mrs Adebola said quickly.

"Pets? *That's* not a spider and *that's* not a puppy," said Ms Idris, pointing at each in turn.

Mrs Adebola cocked a brow at her sister. "And just what, exactly, do you think they are?"

"Monsters!" Ms Idris cried. "They're all *monsters*!"

Dexter and his mum looked scandalized. Sherman went rigid. Even Sylvester froze, belly-up on the rug. Theodora felt equally stunned: how could Ms Idris possibly know Sherman and Sylvester were monsters? Sure, neither was glamoured, but there was nothing obviously monsterish about either. Ms Idris had accused Theodora of bringing "more of them" into her home – did this mean she suspected that Mummy, Dracula and Wilhelmina were monsters too? But they *had* been glamoured…

And then Theodora's breath caught in her chest like a firefly trapped in a jar: *could Dexter's aunt see through glamours?*

Whether or not certain humans can see through glamours is a question I've spent many years pondering. Ten long, lonely years. And the answer to this query is very important to the remainder of our tale – but then, I'm getting ahead of myself.

After what could have been a minute or an hour, Dexter's mum fixed a plastic-looking smile onto her face. "How ridiculous!" she said with a forced laugh. "Monsters don't exist."

A muscle in Ms Idris's jaw twitched. "They do, too. For goodness' sake, you let Dexter run amuck with a whole family of them!"

"Dexter doesn't run *amuck*—"

"Call it what you want," Ms Idris interrupted. "But your son is regularly in the company of dangerous monsters! I know you can see them," she added. "Why deny it?"

Dexter's mum hesitated. Theodora had the feeling

she was doing some very quick thinking. But then, Theodora was doing some very quick thinking of her own: as she waited for Mrs Adebola's reply, she started remembering things. Things she'd thought were strange at the time – odd, even – but which now suddenly seemed to make sense.

How Mrs Adebola was the only human who didn't seem uncomfortable around Theodora's family, never instinctively backing away from Mummy, never shivering when Dracula walked past. How she was the only grown-up in all of Appleton who allowed her child to visit 13 Battington Lane unsupervised. How, when a golden bird had leaked from a wound on Mummy's shoulder and landed upon the rim of her glass at the party at Halloween, Mrs Adebola had acted as if it was merely a neat little parlour trick...

"You can, can't you?" Theodora said, breaking the silence. "You can see monsters – I mean, you can see through their glamours."

"C-can you?" asked Dexter, staring at his mother in amazement; while he had seen Theodora's family in all their monster-glory plenty of times, he'd never been able to see through their glamours as his aunt – and, apparently, his mother – seemed to be able to do.

Before Mrs Adebola could reply, the phone rang. Looking relieved, she swept across the room, placing the receiver against her ear. "Idris residence," she said, then held out the phone to Theodora. "It's for you, dear."

"Theodora?" came Mummy's frantic voice over the line. "Are you OK?"

"We're fine," Theodora replied, releasing a breath she hadn't realized she'd been holding. *Mummy was OK!* "What about you guys?"

"We're fine too," Mummy assured her, though there was something in her tone that made Theodora think she wasn't being completely honest. "Come downstairs, I'm here."

"OK," she agreed, hanging up the phone. "My mummy's downstairs," Theodora told the room at large.

"Then let's not keep her waiting," Sherman said, speaking for the first time.

Ms Idris jumped at the sound of his voice, though Mrs Adebola didn't seem the least bit surprised that the well-dressed tarantula sitting upon Theodora's shoulder could talk.

"I just have one question," Theodora said, dividing her gaze evenly between Dexter's mum and aunt. "Have you told anyone that you can see monsters?"

Ms Idris let out a snort. "Of course not," she said. "Besides – who'd believe us if we did?"

The Vampire's Lament

Time for another recap, I think.

We now know that the source of the so-called incidents at the New York MLM were the Shadowmongers, who'd aligned themselves with Hilda in exchange for their freedom. At Hilda's direction, they'd struck both a witch and a vampire, and now poor Boolivia D'Ghoul, before making their appearance at the Monster UN. If you've been paying close attention, you might have noticed that the name listed in Boolivia's diary, Thelda H. Gaih, is an anagram of "Hilda the Hag". (For those of you sleeping through your English lessons, an anagram is a phrase formed by rearranging the letters of another word or phrase.) We also know that the Shadowmongers have terrible effects on their victims, causing monsters to lose their powers and humans to suffer eternal

nightmares – which poor Theodora would face that very evening. But perhaps the most shocking discovery we've made is that Dexter's mum can see through glamours – something I have long suspected to be true.

But now, we have other matters to which we need to attend.

"Mummy!" Theodora cried, throwing her arms around her waist. "You're OK!"

"I'm fine," a freshly glamoured Mummy assured her. "How about you three?"

"We're all fine," Sherman replied.

Theodora did not correct him. Something about Mummy's pinched expression was making her anxious. She wanted to get back to the Manhattan MLM and see for herself that the others were unharmed.

"Thank darkness. Harriet is packing our things and the others are waiting for us back at the hotel,"

Mummy said, urging them into the waiting taxi.

"Is everyone OK?" Theodora wanted to know. "I saw a Shadowmonger hit Wilhelmina..."

"Don't worry about Wilhelmina," Mummy assured her, though Theodora couldn't help but notice that she was avoiding her gaze. "Now, I've booked us on the next train home."

"But we're supposed to be here for another week," Theodora said in surprise. "Mrs Adebola was going to take me and Dexter to the Museum of Natural History tomorrow..."

"Not any more," Mummy said grimly. "Headquarters has ordered all MLM members back to their bases to await further instructions."

"But why?"

"I imagine it's safer for everyone to scatter," Sherman reasoned. "I mean, look what happened at the UN – we don't want to find ourselves sitting ducks again."

The journey back to London was very different from the one to New York, sombre and quiet. Miles, the *Glass Express*'s crocoman barman, tried to cheer them up with an offer of free chocolate milkshakes (my favourite!), but even that couldn't brighten the mood. The little group soon arrived back in the Hall of

Reflection, which, unlike their last visit, was completely devoid of monsters – except for Helter-Skelter.

"Where is everyone?" Theodora asked the skeleton.

"On duty: they're working to ensure that the mansion has the highest level of security, what with Hilda and those frightful Shadowmongers on the loose."

"Helter-Skelter, can you please give Sylvester a bath?" asked Mummy, holding the wriggling cub away from her wrappings. "I don't know *what* he rolled in."

"Of course," the butler agreed solicitously, taking the offending pup into his arms.

"We need to fill the others in," said Dracula, stepping through the mirror and joining them in the corridor.

"I'll be there in a minute," replied Wilhelmina, who, it must be said, looked rather awful: her skin was sallow, muted to a sickly sage instead of its usual vibrant evergreen.

"Let me make you a pot of tea before I bathe Sylvester," Helter-Skelter offered kindly.

"Thanks, but I think I'm in need of something stronger," Wilhelmina said without breaking stride. "Besides," she added, patting her pocket, "I want to take Grimeny Cricket to his room..."

"Poor Wilhelmina," Sherman said as she rounded the corner.

Poor Wilhelmina, indeed. The witch had lost her powers. She could no longer cast spells, or brew potions, or saddle her broom for a midnight flight around the moon. I'm sure I don't need to tell you how truly awful it is to be a witch without magic – and I don't mean awful like when your Auntie Mae knits you an ugly, itchy Christmas jumper and your parents make you wear it for the entire day; I mean awful like when you find out that your very best friend is moving to the other side of the country – that sort of awful.

"I made a platter of sandwiches if you're hungry," Helter-Skelter said to Theodora and Sherman, as Mummy and Dracula hurried off too. "Help yourselves – I'd best get this one in the tub," he said, nodding at Sylvester, who'd started gnawing on his collarbone.

Not knowing what else to do, Theodora and Sherman made their way into the kitchen where, as promised, a platter of sandwiches sat on the counter. Theodora pulled off the plastic wrap, grabbing a ham and cheese sandwich for herself and a turkey sandwich for Sherman, slathering it in his favourite strawberry jam.

"Aren't you going to eat?" she asked, noticing that he hadn't taken a single bite.

"I'm not very hungry," he said mournfully, wiping one of his monocles. "I can't stop thinking about those

Shadowmongers. Boolivia's been transformed into a doll and Grimeny Cricket's become mute and poor Wilhelmina has lost her magic…"

"It's terrible," Theodora agreed, dropping the sandwich to the plate; suddenly she wasn't hungry either.

"I think I'll turn in early. I could use a good night's rest."

"I'll be up in a bit," said Theodora. She had no desire to go to sleep just yet.

And who can blame her? If I knew I'd have terrible nightmares every time I closed my eyes from now until kingdom come, I don't think I'd be in a rush to go to bed either.

The next day – Christmas Eve – the monsters were on high alert, having received notice from Headquarters that Hilda and the Shadowmongers were on the loose. They were taking turns patrolling the premises and guarding the entrances. Dracula made a rare appearance at breakfast (vampires aren't typically morning-monsters), having just completed an overnight shift. "Hello," he said gloomily, slumping onto a stool at the kitchen counter.

"Are you all right?" asked Sherman, peering at him over the top of his monocles. "You look a bit peaky."

"Fine," he replied shortly.

"Are you quite sure?"

"Yes – no," Dracula admitted. "It's just, our trip ended a bit abruptly..."

"Well, no one knew that Hilda was going to show up with a bunch of Shadowmongers," said Wilhelmina, sweeping into the kitchen. "I'll take that tea now, please," she added to Helter-Skelter.

"Earl Grey or English Breakfast?" he enquired, popping the kettle onto the stove.

"The latter, I think."

"How are you feeling, Wilhelmina?" asked an equally peaky-looking Theodora; just as we'd feared, she'd had terrible dreams the entire night: in one, Boolivia, still in marionette form, was performing on stage, Hilda pulling her strings like a puppet master.

In another, Grimeny Cricket was hopping through the soft, tall strands of grass that lined a pond when a frog's tongue snapped through the air, swallowing him whole. In yet another, a furious Wilhelmina was screaming at Theodora that she'd lost her powers for nothing… It was, as you can imagine, simply awful; Theodora felt completely unrested.

Wilhelmina ignored the question. "What's wrong with you?" she asked Dracula abruptly.

"Nothing."

"Dracula, we've known each other for over three centuries – I know when something's wrong. Spit it out."

"It's just… I was hoping to take Mummy to dinner at Eleven Madison Bark before we left New York. They make a lovely Houndstooth's pudding – her favourite, you know."

Wilhelmina's eyebrows shot to the top of her head. "You're not upset because Hilda's trying to take over Headquarters with the help of the foulest creatures to ever roam the earth – and doing a decent job of it, I might add – but because *you didn't get to take Mummy to dinner*?" This time, Wilhelmina couldn't resist rolling her eyes. "Well, why don't you take her

out around here?" she suggested. "There are plenty of excellent restaurants in London."

"I suppose. Though this probably isn't the best time to ask her..."

Wilhelmina stared at him in disbelief. "All this moping about and you haven't even *asked* her? Oh, this is going to take for ever," she said, shaking her head.

Theodora's brow furrowed: *what* was going to take for ever? But before she could ask there was a tapping at the window, where a bird had perched on the sill. For one heart-stopping moment, Theodora thought it was the skele-crow, returned to its normal size. But its feathers were not the black of an inkpot but the white of a lily – besides, this bird had a letter clasped in its beak: it was Owen, the ghostly MLM post owl.

Out of habit, Wilhelmina pulled out her wand and gave it a wave. Of course, nothing happened. Throwing the wand down in disgust, she strode across the room and flung the window open. Owen soared across the kitchen, dropping the envelope in front of Dracula.

"Urgent letter from Headquarters," he said, ruffling his feathers importantly.

Dracula tore the envelope open, scanning its contents.

"What is it?" asked Theodora.

"More Shadowmonger attacks. And not just in New York. There are similar reports coming out of the Barcelona MLM and the Tokyo MLM."

"That's terrible," tsked Helter-Skelter, topping up Wilhelmina's tea.

"It gets worse," Dracula said, the shadows under his eyes darkening to the colour of overripe blackberries. "Apparently, Hilda's been sighted at six different MLM agencies in the past twenty-four hours."

"How?" Sherman wanted to know. "That's impossible!"

“How, indeed?” Dracula wondered as he got to his feet, slipping the letter inside his cape. He wandered out of the room, apparently lost in thought.

“I’d best head back to the post office,” said Owen, taking off through the window.

“Wish I could go for a flight,” Wilhelmina said broodingly.

Theodora glanced at Sherman, unsure how to comfort the witch. He shook his head. Sometimes, there just aren’t any words, and this was one of those times.

All That Glitters Is Not Goldie

Christmas dawned a soft, pale pink. Theodora could just make out the bats – yes, *bats* – swooping about her room. They hadn't been there when she'd gone to bed, so she figured Dracula had sent them after she fell asleep. And although the constant flapping of their leathery wings interrupted the early-morning quiet, Theodora did not mind their presence; in fact, she found it rather comforting. The same couldn't be said for Sherman, who sighed every time one of the critters landed on the nightstand, invariably knocking over a glass of water or sending the alarm clock crashing to the floor.

After Sherman's fifth or sixth sigh, Theodora flung off her covers and rolled out of bed. She'd had another terrible night, this time dreaming that Mummy had decided she didn't want her any more and was sending her off to live with Ms Frumple.

You're wondering why Theodora hadn't told anyone that she'd been attacked by the Shadowmongers? A fair question. The reason was, in a word: Wilhelmina. The witch had lost her powers because she'd chosen to protect Theodora – how could she look her in the eye and tell her it was all for nothing? Besides, there was no known cure for the Shadowmongers' curse – what was the point in bringing it up?

Shaking her head to clear it of these troubling thoughts, Theodora moseyed over to her desk. She picked up her torat deck, idly wondering as she shuffled the cards if the golden-haired woman was still moving about. Theodora wasn't left pondering for long, for the first card she selected was *The Lady. Or was it?* The illustration no longer featured the golden-haired woman, but the brunette from *The Empress* card, sullen-faced and cross-armed.

"The Lady!" Sherman exclaimed, peering at the card from her shoulder. "She's gone!"

"But where?" Theodora mused, tossing down the second card.

"*The Moon*," Sherman said. "Nightmares. Things that go bump in the night. Again."

"That certainly fits," Theodora murmured, flipping over the final card: *The Empress*. "At least we've found the golden-haired woman," she said.

And sure enough, the woman who had previously featured on *The Lady* card was now occupying the throne depicted in *The Empress* card; it seemed the blonde and the brunette had swapped places. But while the dark-haired woman was as still as a statue, the golden-haired woman was anything but: she seemed to be beating her fists against the front of the card as if she were trying to break free of it.

"This isn't normal torat pack behaviour," said Sherman worriedly. "Even for a deck as, well, *unusual* as yours.

You know, I think it might be time to pay Goldie a visit," he said abruptly. "Let's ask her how to stop the Shadowmongers."

"Good idea," Theodora agreed, glad to have something to do. She shoved her feet into her favourite zombie-bunny slippers. Still in their pyjamas, they strode past the sleeping suits of armour and made their way down the ivory staircase, where some of the eyes winked blearily as they passed.

They arrived at the bare little room, empty apart from the Heads, who were also asleep – except for the rabbit, who said, "You're up early, even for Christmas morning."

"We wanted to wish Goldie Happy Christmas," said Sherman.

"That's nice," said the rabbit. "Goldie doesn't get many visitors – or any, really, except for you two. Go on."

Theodora crossed the room, brushing her fingers against a small tear in the wallpaper. A little round door appeared. She crossed the threshold and began climbing the narrow, winding staircase. Up and up and up they went, past the music chamber where Figaro was already practising his scales and coming to a halt at what *appeared* to be a dead end. Of course, it wasn't dead, for a few moments later a loud, rasping sound filled their ears. Something as thick as a tree trunk was scraping its way down the stone wall. But this was no trunk; it was a massive, metallic-gold tail – a wosnak tail, to be exact.

In case you've forgotten, wosnaks are some of the rarest creatures in the world. They have the body of a cobra and the head of a woman and possess the genie-like ability to grant wishes (alas, ending world hunger and bestowing eternal youth are forbidden). In exchange, they demand one of two forms of payment: a gift (which no one ever chooses because wosnaks are notoriously difficult to shop for) or the correct answer to a riddle.

In the time it took to remind you of all of this, the wosnak's tail had wound itself around Theodora's waist and hoisted her into the air.

"Theodoraaaa, Sssssssherman," Goldie hissed. "To whaaaat do I owe the pleassssssssssure?"

"Hi, Goldie," said Theodora, patting her

scales in greeting. "Happy Christmas."

The twin balls of fire that were Goldie's eyes blazed with warmth. "Happy Chrissstmassss. But then, you arrrrrre not jussssst here to exchange pleasssssantriessss."

"How did you know that?"

The wosnak smiled, revealing fangs as long as Theodora's forearms. "IIIIIII know allll. Wellll?"

Theodora glanced at Sherman, who nodded encouragingly.

"I'm sure you've already heard – since you know all and everything – but terrible things have been happening. Hilda's back, she's got an army of Shadowmongers and—"

"I knoooooow," Goldie interrupted, eyes burning as fiercely as dying stars.

Theodora and Sherman looked away from the dazzling sight. "We wanted to ask you how to stop the Shadowmongers," she finished.

"How ssssshall you paaaay for the ansssswer?"

"Riddle," said Sherman confidently; he was good at solving puzzles.

"Verrrrry wellllll. Riddddddle me thisssss:

"Some may hang me on the wall,
look upon my face and bawl.
For I reveal no more or less,
than time's own passing, I confess.
My image changes, that is true.
This, then, is my final clue:
your reflection I do show,
but who you are, I'll never know.
What am I?"

"Hmm," said Sherman, scratching his hairy chin with his even hairier leg. "Time's own passing… Hang me on the wall. That could be a clock? No, that's not my answer!"

Goldie didn't reply, merely watching the tarantula with mild interest.

"*My image changes*… What does that mean?"

Something clicked in Theodora's mind. "It's a mirror," she said, surprised at her own cleverness. "*Your reflection I do show, but who you are I'll never know!* A mirror can show who you are on the outside, but not who you are on the inside!"

"Corrrrect," said Goldie, hood flaring in pleasure.

As she spoke, a silver-plated mirror appeared out of thin air. Theodora's face stared back at her, pale and perturbed.

"A mirror? How's a mirror supposed to stop the Shadowmongers?" asked Sherman.

But Goldie did not reply. The mirror vanished, and Theodora felt herself being lowered to the floor; their audience with the wosnak was over.

"Well, that wasn't what I expected," said Sherman.

"Me neither," Theodora replied. "We must be missing something..."

And, of course, they were.

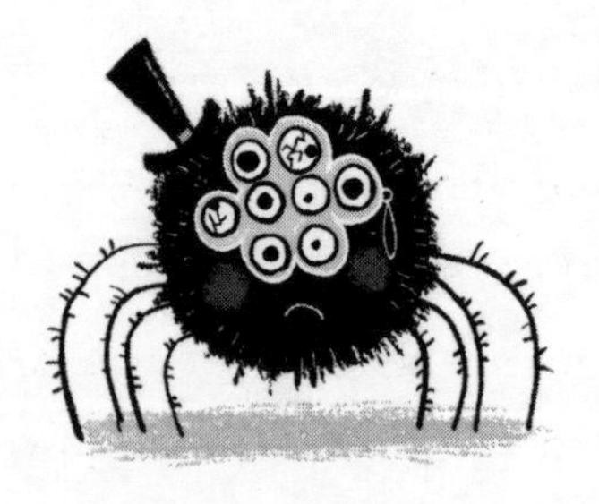

The Most Villainous Villain's Revenge

Christmas was a subdued affair; no one felt much like celebrating. After opening presents beneath the tree, everyone retired to the dining room for a delicious – if restrained – luncheon.

And the next week, their New Year's Eve celebration would be just as quiet. The monsters weren't even planning to host their annual bash: there had been a number of attacks on MLM agencies across the globe by Hilda and the Shadowmongers (though how Hilda was managing to get from one side of the world to the other in the blink of an eye remained a mystery), and many good monsters now found themselves powerless – or worse – as a result. In an attempt to prevent further losses, Headquarters had advised all MLM members to remain indoors as much as possible while the Shadowmongers were still at large.

As for Theodora, she was spending a lot of time indoors too – mainly because she was so exhausted from her daily nightmares that she didn't have the energy to do more than laze about: her head felt heavy and fuzzy, her eyeballs dry and bleary. She'd grown nearly as pale as Dracula, and the shadows beneath her eyes were nearly as dark as those that darkened the vampire's face. And worse, the monsters were starting to notice: Helter-Skelter insisted on making her warm milk to drink before bed, Dracula had taken to reading her a bedtime story like he used to do when she was small, and Mummy had made her bedtime one whole hour earlier – not that any of this helped.

By the time New Year's Eve rolled around, Theodora was rather like a zombie. Yawning widely, she shuffled into the Beelzebub Parlour, where the residents of 13 Battington Lane had gathered. Helter-Skelter had decorated the room with hundreds of flickering candles and set up several buffet tables fit to groaning with a variety of sweets and savouries in an effort to cheer everyone up.

"Happy New Year!" the butler cried when the clock

struck twelve, tossing handfuls of confetti into the air.

"Happy New Year," the monsters dutifully replied. They exchanged the requisite hugs and platitudes, assuring one another that the coming year would be better than the last – it had to be.

Dracula sidled up to Mummy. "Happy New Year," he said shyly.

"Happy New Year!" she replied, giving him a peck on the cheek.

Dracula looked like a deer in the headlights, gingerly touching the place where Mummy's lips had brushed against his icy skin. "Mummy," he said suddenly, "would you like to go to dinner with me this week?"

"As in, just the two of us?" she asked uncertainly.

He nodded.

The corners of Mummy's mouth quirked into a smile. "Go on, then."

Dracula grinned, fangs gleaming in the candlelight. "How about nine o'clock on Saturday? We can't go out, obviously, but I'll ask Helter-Skelter to prepare something special."

"It's a date," Mummy said. She moved to join the trolls, who were celebrating their Reform School graduation to ***Reform Level Nine:*** *Personal Accountability*

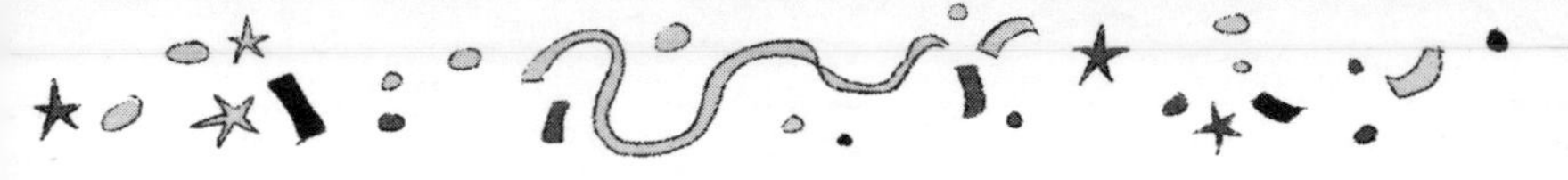

in a Monstrously Tempting World.

Still beaming, Dracula sauntered off in search of a celebratory glass of blood.

"Well," said Wilhelmina, who'd been watching their exchange from the armchair nearest the blazing fire, "that's progress, I suppose."

"Precious little," said Sir Pumpkin-de-Patch, taking a sip of pumpkin juice. "He's liked her for what, two hundred years?"

"Let's just hope that Headquarters is quicker at catching Shadowmongers than Dracula was at asking Mummy out," Marty said darkly.

Before Theodora knew it, the holidays had come to an end. The new term would begin the next day and, for the first time ever, Theodora found that she was looking forward to going back to school. It wasn't that she was eager to return to Appleton Primary – not exactly. She just couldn't stand being stuck in the mansion any longer. The monsters, who'd been trapped indoors for several weeks, were all on edge, exhausted as they took turns on guard duty, or worked on tracking Hilda's whereabouts, or tried to assist the MLM scholars who were researching antidotes to the Shadowmongers' effects. It didn't help that letters arrived from Headquarters several times a day, bearing increasingly terrible news.

Hilda spotted in three different cities over the course of two hours.

SIX MEMBERS of the Brussels MLM attacked by **Shadowmongers.**

The Hamburg MLM walls have been breached;
multiple casualties reported.

The next day, a permanently exhausted Theodora barely managed to get out of bed, arriving at school just as the final bell trilled. She was hurrying towards the Year Five classroom when she was approached by Ms Frumple.

"Well, Ms Hendrix," said the head teacher, skipping over the pleasantries as usual. "I assume you have your completed family tree ready for me to look at?"

Theodora's heart stopped. Curses! With everything that had been going on she'd completely forgotten about that stupid assignment. Swallowing hard (there was no way this was going to end well), Theodora mumbled something in reply.

"What's that?" asked Ms Frumple, cupping a hand around her ear in an exaggerated fashion.

"No, ma'am."

A smirk slid across the head teacher's face. "Well, I can't say I'm surprised. Come with me, Ms Hendrix."

Once again, Theodora and Ms Frumple made the trek to the head teacher's office in silence. The room looked as sterile as ever: no Christmas cards were strung up on the walls, no jar of cookies sat on the desk. Unsurprised by this (Ms Frumple seemed to despise anything that other people might consider fun, let alone festive), Theodora flopped into her usual chair while Ms Frumple sat down behind her desk.

"Why didn't you complete your assignment?" she began without preamble.

Theodora shrugged. What could she say? Obviously, she couldn't reveal that her family was made up of monsters. She supposed she could explain that she was adopted and knew nothing about her original family, but she couldn't bring herself to share this: Ms Frumple just wasn't the sort of grown-up who invited such confidences. Perhaps it was the coldness of her smile, or the way she delighted in handing out detentions. Or maybe it was because Theodora knew that Ms Frumple couldn't care less about anyone else's thoughts or feelings – especially if they diverged from her own. (She really is the worst villain of all time.)

"You are officially suspended," Ms Frumple said with relish. "You will spend the next three days with me, here, copying lines," she added, passing Theodora a book ominously titled *An Instructor's Guide to Encouraging Student Obedience*. "I will tell Mrs Dullson not to expect you in class before Thursday. Take out your notebook."

Now, I don't know if you've ever been set lines, but I have. It's terribly dull work; I would rather get stung by a jellyfish or made to eat smelly, rubbery Brussels sprouts every day for a month than copy lines. And poor Theodora was in for three whole days of it.

Time moved as slowly as a snail sliming its way down a garden path. Theodora couldn't help glancing at the clock every few minutes, which seemed to be ticking so slowly she wondered if it had stopped working altogether. When the lunch bell finally rang, she gleefully threw down her pen. She couldn't wait to catch up with Dexter, whom she hadn't seen since her untimely exit from New York.

But Ms Frumple had other ideas. "Where do you think you're going, young lady?" she asked.

"To lunch, ma'am."

"Oh, no," she replied with a little laugh that set Theodora's teeth on edge. "You'll eat in here with me. Did you bring a packed lunch, or shall I ask Mr Jackson to fetch you something from the lunch hall?"

Any hopes Theodora had that the next two days would go any better were quickly dashed: each day was more brutal than the last. Having gone without a good night's rest for nearly three weeks, Theodora was having even more trouble concentrating on her school work than usual. Ms Frumple was quick to point out any mistakes, forcing Theodora to scratch out the messier pages and begin again. And by the time she finally reached the end of her suspension, her hand so cramped and curled she doubted it would ever fully straighten again.

"A moment, Ms Hendrix," Ms Frumple said at the end of the afternoon on Wednesday as Theodora moved to leave. "I want to make sure that you and I understand one another."

"Ma'am?"

"It's a matter of physics, Ms Hendrix. Every action has an equal and opposite reaction. When you break a rule, that act elicits a punishment that is its equal and opposite reaction. You broke a rule, and your punishment was an in-school suspension with me. Any further rule-breaking will result in additional punishments leading up to and including expulsion. I told you," she said suddenly, "you won the battle when you and your little gang protested against my proposals to improve this school, but I shall win the war."

Ms Frumple was just as good – or perhaps I should say, bad – as her word: when Theodora showed up late to school the following Monday (having endured another torturous, nightmare-filled sleep), Ms Frumple cornered her in the corridor and gave her some extra homework – science homework, to be exact: she was to make a Shadow Catcher.

"What's that?" Theodora asked.

"A Shadow Catcher is a simple device that

demonstrates how shadows work. It's essentially a cardboard box with a large square cut out of the cardboard. A piece of contact paper is then taped across the back. The box should be placed in front of a light source. A torch, a candle or the like. When an object is placed between the light source and the contact paper, a shadow will appear. When the object is withdrawn, the shadow will vanish. You have two weeks."

"Ma'am, would it be possible for me to do some other assignment?" Theodora ventured. "Maybe something to do with English, or History, or—"

"Oh, no," Ms Frumple said with a cold, calculating smile. "Mrs Dullson said you've been struggling to pay attention during Science. This will be a good opportunity indeed to help you regain your focus."

"OK." Theodora sighed; it wasn't worth explaining that she was currently struggling to pay attention in *all* her lessons, given how tired she was. Admittedly, she did find Science to be the least interesting of her subjects and was indeed finding it difficult to stay awake during her lessons – how typical of Ms Frumple to figure out what subject Theodora liked the least before fixing her punishment.

"It's so unfair," Dexter sympathized at lunchtime.

"Since when has Frumple ever been fair?" Theodora replied, popping a crisp into her mouth.

"Good point. If you want, I can help you make the Shadow Catcher next weekend."

"That would be great," Theodora said, relieved. Unlike her, Dexter greatly enjoyed their Science lessons and would undoubtedly be a great help. "Thanks."

"Have you told your parents about this?" Ella wanted to know, looking up from the book she was reading.

Theodora shook her head.

"Why not?"

She shrugged.

"I really think you should," Ella pressed. "My grandpa would be furious if I was getting extra homework every week for such petty crimes."

"Maybe we should protest again," suggested Billy, who was always down for stirring up trouble – especially if it came at Ms Frumple's cost.

"Really, it's fine," said Theodora.

"It's not fine," Ella said hotly, casting her book aside. "I mean, if I were you, I would just try to follow the rules a bit more, but that's not the—"

"Just drop it, OK?" Theodora exploded. "I'm sick of talking about this!" She leapt to her feet and stormed out of the lunch hall. She wasn't heading anywhere particular and found herself walking aimlessly around the school, not paying particular attention to where she was going. Some minutes later, she found herself standing in front of the gym. It wasn't her favourite place, but she decided to go in anyway: it was much too cold for the playground. She settled on a bench in the corner, not far from where some Year Six kids were playing a game of basketball.

Now that she was alone, Theodora was starting to feel ashamed of her outburst. She hadn't meant to yell at Ella – after all, it wasn't her fault that Theodora was about to get kicked out of school, she'd only been trying to help. But if she was being perfectly honest, Theodora didn't *want* Ella's help; she didn't need advice from someone who didn't think she was good enough to invite to her birthday party.

And while we're on the subject, Theodora was well and truly sick of hearing about that. The party was coming up in two weeks' time, and it seemed to be all that anyone could talk about. She couldn't help feeling that it was insensitive for everyone to keep mentioning it in front of her, seeing as she was apparently the only one who wasn't invited. Theodora especially wanted to say something to Dexter, but couldn't bring herself to do so. What if he brushed her off or got angry – or worse, thought she was a crybaby? What if he decided she wasn't cool enough to hang out with any more? It was too awful to contemplate.

Little did Theodora know that a birthday party would soon be the least of her increasingly long list of worries.

At that very moment, Owen was tapping his beak

against the kitchen window. Helter-Skelter opened it, accepting the letter he proffered and promising to deliver it to Dracula directly. Helter-Skelter scurried off, forgetting to close the window in his haste – a thoughtless, innocent act that would have terrible – no, tremendous – no, titanic – consequences. A few minutes later, a small, shadowy *something* seeped into the kitchen through the still-open window, drifting across the room and down the hallway…

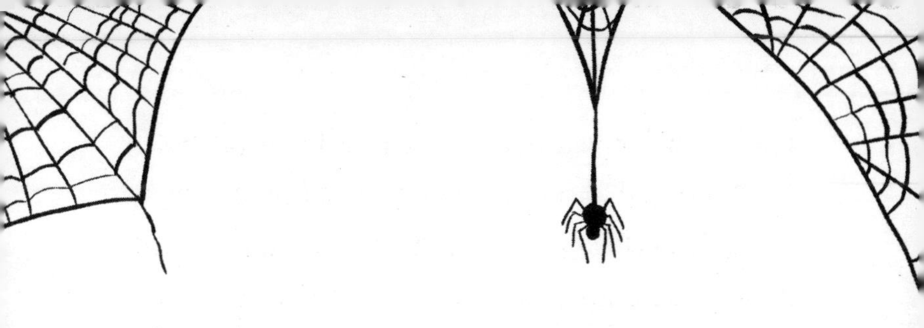

Double, Double, Toil and Trouble

That weekend, Theodora and Sherman headed to the library. Determined to avoid any more punishment from Ms Frumple, Theodora was going to spend the afternoon looking up examples of Shadow Catchers. She walked past the rows of books, pausing before a once-grand mahogany desk that sat at the back of the room. Sitting atop its chipped, scratched surface was a black-flame candle, the usual assortment of books, and Hamlet, the skull. Perched beside him was Mousetrap, the raven. As I'm sure you recall, Hamlet and Mousetrap are the librarians, responsible for cataloguing and maintaining the mansion's vast collection of books in addition to guarding the hidden entrance to the mausoleum. (I told you, a place as haunted as 13 Battington Lane is fit to bursting with secret passageways.)

"Hi, Hamlet, Mousetrap," Theodora said.

Neither responded.

"Hamlet? Mousetrap?"

Silence.

"Theodora," Sherman finally said in a hushed voice. "Something's wrong."

Theodora eyed the librarians. They were unusually still – Mousetrap wasn't even fidgeting. She waited a beat, thinking they must be teasing her. But as the seconds ticked past, she realized this was no game. Sherman was right: something was very, very wrong.

"Sherman," she said, a lump forming in the back of her throat, "they're..."

"… gone," he finished, all eight of his milky eyes glistening with tears.

And indeed they were. The librarians had been reduced to mere objects: Hamlet was now a motionless, expressionless skull while Mousetrap was nothing more than a stuffed bird.

"Theodora, you don't think this could be the work of Shadowmongers, do you?"

"I do," said Theodora, nodding. "But how did they get in? After the skele-crow escaped, Marty put in all sorts of extra security measures – and the whole MLM have been working round the clock to make sure nothing can get into the mansion."

"I don't know, but we should get out of here – what if they're still around?"

Theodora shivered. The Shadowmongers had already got her, damning her to a lifetime of nightmares – she had the mottled, bruised-looking circles under her eyes to prove it – but she *wouldn't* let them get Sherman. "Let's go," she said, turning her back on the librarians; there was nothing she could do for them now. They hastened towards the kitchen, where Helter-Skelter was preparing dinner.

"Have you seen Mummy?" Theodora asked.

"She's in the pumpkin patch, but—"

"Thanks!" she yelled, hurtling towards the garden. She arrived to find Mummy, Dracula, Marty, Georgie and Bandit huddled together in the middle of the garden.

"Mummy," Theodora cried, "something's happened to— What's wrong?" she asked, catching sight of Mummy's tear-streaked face. A feeling of dread bubbled up from the pit of Theodora's stomach: she'd never seen Mummy cry before. Something really awful must have happened.

"It's Sir Pumpkin-de-Patch," Mummy said in a shaking voice. She stepped aside. Behind her was some sort of … scarecrow. A scarecrow made of thick, twisted vines instead of the usual straw. It had a pumpkin for a head with mismatched eyes carved into the flesh of the gourd…

Sherman turned away, but Theodora looked Mummy straight in the eye, and said, "He's not the only one the Shadowmongers have got."

"Meow?" Bandit asked. Here, I think, he meant, "Who's been hurt?"

"The librarians," Sherman said sadly. "They've been turned into objects."

Marty let out a string of curses so filthy it made Mummy say, "Not in front of Theodora!"

"Just wait until I get my hands on that hag," the werewolf growled. "I'm going to tear her limb from limb..."

"Eurga," Georgie agreed, an unusually ugly look upon his face.

"I'll inform Headquarters," Dracula sighed. "That's all I seem to be doing these days... Marty, we need to do a sweep of the premises, see if anyone else has been affected."

Marty nodded, heading back into the mansion. Theodora spared Sir Pumpkin-de-Patch one last look. A magpie, undeterred by the dummy whose sole purpose was to scare him off, landed on the scarecrow's outstretched arm. Theodora couldn't help but think this was a bad omen.

How very right she was.

The residents of 13 Battington Lane were as unnerved as Theodora had ever seen them: Wilhelmina was listless, Bon was barely eating while Georgie was overeating (consuming a shocking amount of candy-floss), and Gabe hadn't left the cellar for days. But the change in Marty was perhaps the most alarming: the werewolf MLM Head of Security was in a positively foul temper, prowling around the property for signs of Hilda and the Shadowmongers, growling at anyone who dared suggest he take a break. Despite their usual bickering, it seemed he was taking Sir Pumpkin-de-Patch's absence very hard indeed.

"The MLM scholars are researching around the clock to find an antidote to the Shadowmongers' effects," Mummy kept assuring him. "With a little luck they'll find one soon."

"They never have before," Marty would grouse. "That's part of why the Shadowmongers were banished in the first place..." the werewolf would trail off, wandering away in a mood as black as the night.

"And they're no c-closer to c-catching Hilda?"

Dexter asked Theodora one blustery Saturday evening. They were sitting on the floor in her room, putting the finishing touches on Theodora's Shadow Catcher – at least, Dexter was. Theodora hadn't done a whole lot more than pass Dexter materials as he requested them. Indeed, he seemed to be enjoying himself, happily admiring his handiwork while munching on a plate of Helter-Skelter's ooey, gooey brownies. (I don't care what anyone says, the middle pieces are better than the edges.)

"No," she said sadly.

"I'd like to think that things will get better soon, but somehow I don't think so," Sherman chipped in.

"Why d-do you say that?"

"The cards."

Dexter looked at Theodora questioningly.

"He means the torat cards," she explained. "They've been acting weird. Well, weirder. Here, I'll show you. See this?" she asked, pulling a card from the middle of the deck, *The Lady*. "Normally, there's a blonde woman on this card. But now there's a brunette."

"I c-can't see anything," said Dexter. "They j-just look like regular c-cards."

"Part of their magic," Sherman said wisely.

"And the blonde woman – see how she's moving around? – is now on the— Ouch!" she cried, dropping the second card she'd selected, *The Empress*. Her thumb felt hot, as if she had placed it against a boiling kettle. A blister was already beginning to form.

"Is something burning?" Dexter asked, sniffing the air.

Indeed it was: tendrils of smoke were unfurling from *The Empress* card, a spark appearing on one corner. Before Theodora could do more than blink in surprise – where had it come from? – the ember grew into a small, flickering flame.

"Fire!" Dexter cried, scooping up the Shadow Catcher and backing away from the flames.

At the same time, Sherman yelled, "The Lady –

she's going to burn up!"

He was right: the golden-haired woman was cowering from the growing blaze as the flames hungrily licked their way across the card. Theodora jumped to her feet, hoping to put out the fire by stomping on it, but she was too late. The card was now totally consumed by the flames. There was a bang like a gunshot, and just like that the fire went out. In place of the blaze, in a pile of ash, stood a golden-haired woman. She was long and lithe and wore powder-blue robes, which were now covered in soot. Her hair was singed and smoking slightly and her face was smudged with ash, but it was her eyes that drew Theodora's attention: they were the exact shade of grass-green as her own.

"That was most unpleasant," said the woman, dusting off her robes. "Though not nearly as unpleasant as being stuck in a deck of cards for ten years..." She shook out her curls, scattering ash all over the carpet. "But I must say, it's lovely to see you again, Theodora."

Theodora gave a start at the use of her name. "Have we met?" she asked uncertainly.

"Oh, yes," the woman replied, eyes sparkling.

Before Theodora could ask when, there was another boom, more of a cannon than a gunshot. The floor began to shake, a couple of figurines toppling off her bookshelf and crashing to the floor.

"E-earthquake?" asked Dexter, looking as if he had seen a ghost – and he had, for Figaro had just floated into the room.

"Theeeee mansion is underrrrr attaaaaaaack!" he sang. "Nooooo ghoooost or ghoooooul or weeeee

spider is saaaafeeee. Ruuuuuuuuuuun for your livessssssssssssssss!"

And with that he drifted out the opposite wall. Theodora watched through the window as Figaro glided over the garden past the scarecrow that was Sir Pumpkin-de-Patch, his outstretched arms now full of six or seven black-and-white birds.

"Magpies," the woman muttered, following Theodora's gaze. "A bad omen… We need to find Mummy. Let's go to the mausoleum – the monsters will probably head there."

"How do you know about the monsters?" asked Sherman.

At the same time, Theodora asked, "How do you know about the mausoleum?"

"You hear things, living in a deck of cards. Come," said the woman, urging the children out the door and down the hallway. They'd nearly reached the staircase when one of the suits of armour that lined the hallway leapt out in front of them.

"But you must allow me to escort you," he cried. "We're under attack!"

"We've heard," the woman said drolly, dodging around him and coming to a stop at the top of the staircase. The steps were *moving*, clinking together like piano keys played by unskilled hands. They did not halt as they usually did at the sound of approaching footsteps: the mansion's defences seemed to have been activated.

"H-how do we g-get down?" stammered Dexter.

"Like this," said the woman, gripping the banister in both hands. She swung her legs over the top and pushed off, sailing down the railing as if it were a slide.

Theodora tried to follow her lead but couldn't quite reach.

"Need a boost?" asked the suit, lifting her onto the banister with one iron hand.

"Thanks," she said, as he gave her a push. Down she went, landing neatly at the bottom of the stairs. Dexter followed, though his landing was not quite as smooth; he fell face-first to the floor.

"Ow," he said, as he got to his feet.

"Are you OK?" asked Sherman in concern.

"Never mind that," said the Lady, her eyes fixed on something further down the hallway. "We've got bigger fish to fry."

As she was speaking, Theodora spotted said fish: a Shadowmonger, slinking towards them from the kitchen. And not just any Shadowmonger – it was the mean little monkey who'd struck Grimeny Cricket and Wilhelmina at the Monster UN. "You can see it?" she asked the woman in surprise.

"Yes," she confirmed shortly, a shadow crossing her pretty features.

They turned in the opposite direction and hurried through the hallway, which looked to be the scene of a recent struggle: a silver tray was overturned on the floor, surrounded by shattered glass. The doors to the coat cupboard had been ripped off their hinges (the very-much-alive mink stole who lived inside it was nowhere to be seen, having traded his hanger for the relative safety of a hat box), and the umbrella stand inlaid with human fingernails had been knocked over. Beside it was a pile of bones – a pile of bones half-buried inside a well-tailored suit and black, glossy shoes…

"Helter-Skelter!" Theodora cried.

But the butler did not – could not – reply.

"Come, now," the woman said, leading them down a darkened hallway, the candelabras having winked out. They had nearly arrived at the Hall of Reflection when Theodora saw something that stopped her in her tracks – it would have stopped you in yours, too.

Fair Is Fowl and Fowl Is Fair

"I do love that *Glass Express*," said Hilda, emerging from the mirrored wall and stepping into the corridor.

"*That's* how she's been managing to be in different cities on the same day!" said Sherman, slapping a leg against his forehead. "How did we miss it?"

I must say, I quite agree; all I can think is that Theodora and her friends – not to mention the MLM – were all so distraught over the fate of the attacked monsters that the thought simply hadn't occurred to them (which is why *we're* on the case, Junior Agent).

"No one's ever accused the MLM of being overly bright," Hilda said baldly. "It was really quite convenient; I've been staying underground with the hobgoblins, you know – nasty things they are – but it was the perfect place to hide the Shadowmongers. Besides, it's much easier to plan for world-wide domination when you're out of sight..."

"That still doesn't explain how she got into the mansion, though," Sherman mused as if she hadn't spoken.

"Oh, I had some help." Hilda grinned.

At that moment, someone else passed through the mirror, stepping into the hallway – someone with a mouthful of sharp, spindly teeth and a lush, handlebar moustache...

"Miles?" Theodora said uncertainly, recognizing the crocoman waiter from the *Glass Express*.

"Indeed," he said, moving to stand beside Hilda.

Theodora's eyes darted between them. "You're working for Hilda?" she gasped. "*You* helped her get inside the mansion – you helped her get into all of the MLM agencies!"

"Only some. The other *Glass Express* bar staff helped too."

"But why?" asked the suit of armour.

"I told you," Hilda interjected. "There are many who think I've got the right idea about things. Oh, but I'm glad you're here, Theodora! I'd hate for you to miss out on the upcoming festivities..."

"What festivities?" the woman from the torat card asked sharply, speaking for the first time since they'd arrived in the Hall of Reflection.

"Althea," said the hag in mock-delight. "Escaped from your cardstock prison, I see? Oh, yes, I know all about you... I have spies everywhere, you know."

The Lady – Althea – straightened, shaking her curls from her eyes. "That was no prison, Hilda, but a place of my own choosing."

"You *chose* t-to live in a d-deck of cards?" Dexter asked in disbelief. "W-why?"

Althea hesitated, and Theodora had the sense that she was choosing her next words carefully. "To protect Theodora," she said slowly.

"Going with half-truths, I see. Now, where's your Mummy?" Hilda asked Theodora. "Or perhaps I should say," she tittered, "where's your *other* mummy?"

"What's that supposed to mean?" Theodora asked, pulse quickening. Out of the corner of her eye, she saw Dexter's head swivelling between her and Althea, a look of dawning comprehension upon his face.

"Never mind," Hilda said dismissively. "What's a paltry family reunion compared to the toppling of the famous London MLM, the last MLM agency on my list? Yes, once the Shadowmongers have dealt with the rest of this snivelling household, I shall be victorious at last! And then you, dearie," she added to Theodora, "will *finally* be my pet."

"Over my dead body," growled Althea, moving towards Theodora.

"Oh, no, you don't!" cried Hilda, whipping her staff through the air. A beam of green light shot from its tip, narrowly missing Althea and striking the mirrored wall just above their heads.

"Run!" cried the suit of armour, throwing himself directly in the path of a second beam. It struck the middle of his chest. He fell to the floor with a clang, a thin stream of smoke issuing from his breastplate.

Theodora made to run over and check on him, but Althea had grabbed her hand and was urging her down the corridor. As they fled the scene, she thought

– or perhaps hoped – she heard the knight groan, but could not be sure… The four of them made a run for it, ducking around corners and along passageways to put as much distance as possible between them and the hag and the crocoman, only coming to a stop when they found their way blocked. The entrance to the library, and with it the secret mausoleum entrance, had completely caved in.

"N-now what?" Dexter gasped.

"This way," said Theodora, dashing for the Ancient Curse Breaking Room. "Come on!" She figured it was as good a place as any to hide – besides, it had *lots* of weapons, and she had a feeling they'd be needing them. She pulled hard on the handle, but the door didn't budge. She groaned with frustration.

"Maybe Goldie can help?" Sherman suggested.

"We've already asked her for help, and all she did was show us a mirror!"

"We need to move along," Althea urged, glancing over her shoulder.

As no one had any better ideas, they raced towards Goldie's tower, listening hard for the sound of footsteps. But all seemed to have gone quiet – in fact, the Heads' room was silent. The reason for this was immediately apparent: the Heads, too, had been caught in the Shadowmongers' snare. They'd been reduced to nothing more than, well, *heads*, sticking blindly, dumbly out of the wall.

Wordlessly, Theodora tickled the tear in the wallpaper and began climbing the stairs. The others followed, halting only when they reached the dead end that marked the start of the wosnak's quarters. This time, Theodora didn't have to wait for Goldie's tail to appear: it was already there, coiled in the corner like a massive, gilded rope.

"Goldie?"

The wosnak did not reply.

"Goldie," Theodora repeated, shaking the wosnak's tail roughly. "Goldie, wake up!"

"I-is she O-OK?"

"Of course she is," Theodora said. But she wasn't as sure as she sounded; Goldie had never kept her waiting before...

"Maybe we should hide somewhere else," Sherman suggested.

"Too late," said Althea. Theodora followed her gaze, and what she saw made the tiny hairs on the back of her neck stand on end: padding slowly up the staircase below them, paws hovering a few centimetres off the floor, was a shadowy pack of wolves.

"Is it the Shadow-m-mongers?" Dexter asked in a shaking voice.

"Yup. On the stairs."

"That means they're blocking the only exit," Sherman groaned. "Oh, I don't want to be turned into a common insect!"

Theodora's chin jutted out in a striking imitation of Mummy when she was about to get her way. "You won't be," she promised, trying to ignore the shadowy creatures slinking in and out of her view, which were now just below them.

"You're a good friend, Theodora," Sherman said softly, "but I'm afraid there's nothing you can do. We're well and truly trapped."

"No, we're not!" she snapped. And then Theodora did something that was either very brave or very stupid – or perhaps a bit of both.

She took a running leap, launching herself onto the wosnak's tail, which resembled nothing so much as a golden, scaly tree trunk, stretching from a coil on the floor to the eaves above, vanishing into the top of the mansion's tallest tower.

"What are you doing?" Sherman cried, barely holding on to his top hat.

"Protecting you from the Shadowmongers," she replied. "Come on!" Using the oversized scales as hand and footholds, Theodora began to climb.

"This is c-crazy," Dexter muttered from below, though Theodora heard him and Althea scrabbling up the wosnak's tail a beat later.

Theodora moved as swiftly as she could, not daring to look behind her. Even so, she could *feel* those hateful creatures prowling around the stairs;

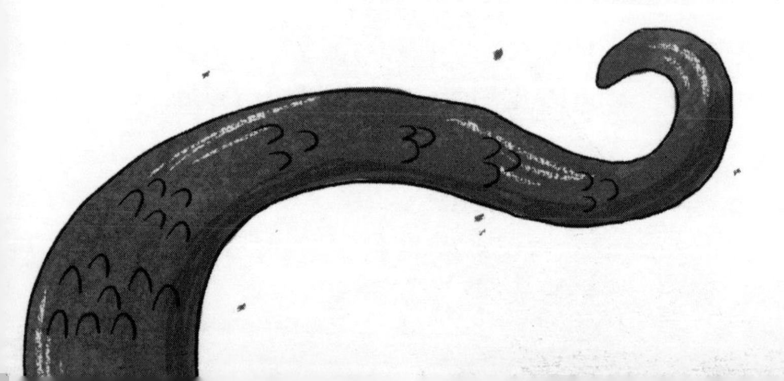

it was only a matter of time before they followed them up the wosnak's tail.

She climbed faster and faster still, pausing only when the tower split into three: two pipes and a chimney. Theodora launched herself into the chimney. If she craned her head just so, she could make out a small patch of sky through the coal-streaked vent. But how to get through it? She wasn't quite tall enough to reach…

"Need a lift?" came Althea's muffled voice below. Theodora felt the Lady's strong, sure hands under her trainers, pushing her upwards.

"Thanks!" Theodora called as she pulled herself up and out of the chimney, squeezing through the sooty pipe and falling onto the roof tiles with a thud.

"Sherman, are you OK?"

"I've broken a monocle," he sighed.

Theodora was about to say she was sorry, but the words died on her lips. She looked around in horror, where she was met with a frightening – no, terrifying – no, horrifying – sight.

A vast array of monsters had gathered at the other end of the roof, their hulking frames only just visible against the black of the night. Amongst the army of creatures were vampires flashing blood-stained fangs; werewolves flexing razor-sharp claws; demons waving lethal-looking spears; massive mummies swinging equally massive scythes; beady-eyed witches twirling their wands between their bony fingers; and dozens upon dozens of hobgoblins, armed with deadly, double-headed axes. They eyed Theodora hungrily as she rose to her feet on legs made of jelly.

"Uh-oh," Dexter said, stumbling out of the chimney and onto the roof behind her.

Althea landed beside him, her gaze sweeping across the terrible scene. "We should go back," she said, paling. She turned back to the chimney, only to find that it had sealed itself shut (another of the mansion's excellent defences).

"W-what are w-we going to do?"

As if in reply, a screeching, squawking sound filled their ears. A dark shape was emerging through the clouds. It was the skele-crow, still magically enlarged. Sitting astride it were Hilda and Miles, his bushy moustache gleaming in the moonlight.

"So lovely to see you all gathered here today," Hilda said as the skele-crow landed in a clatter upon the roof, "waiting to bear witness to the fall of the once-mighty London MLM!"

The crowd cheered in reply, waving their weapons and stomping their feet. Hilda indulged them for a moment, then said, "And then we shall take over Headquarters and announce the new world order – one in which monsters rule over humans!"

The response this time was deafening; Theodora was sure their neighbours must be able to hear the noise. She fervently hoped they would have the good sense to stay at home. Theodora couldn't say that she was especially fond of Mrs Next Door, Mrs Across the Street or Mr Down the Road, but that didn't mean she wanted to see them end up a vampire's supper.

"And behold," Hilda continued, "the MLM's *human* has joined us, just as I hoped! This'll make things easy… If I know the MLM, they'll do anything to protect her. Even if it means meeting their own untimely ends—"

"You're right," called a harsh voice. A voice that filled Theodora with hope and Hilda with fury.
A voice belonging to…

The Macabre MSM

"Mummy," spat the hag. "So glad you could join us."

Mummy was standing on the far side of the roof, perched upon one of its many turrets. Theodora couldn't help thinking that she looked like a comic book superhero: her back was tall and straight, her dark hair blowing in the wind. Her bandaged hands were full of her favourite, deadly knives. She scanned the scene, her fierce gaze softening as it came to rest upon Theodora. "Are you all right?" she asked.

"We're fine. We had help," Theodora said, nodding at Althea.

Mummy did a double take, her mouth forming an "o" of surprise. After a beat, she turned back to Hilda. "I'd ask why you're here," she began, "but you made yourself quite clear at the UN: you want to destroy the MLM, take over Headquarters, and bring monsters out of hiding," she rattled off in a bored-sounding voice.

"Correct. And as you can see, I'm not alone – darkness, no. But you are, Mummy!"

"Meow!"

You're right, of course: it was Bandit, trotting along the narrow roof edge. Here, I think, he meant, "She's not alone, you mean old hag!"

And where Bandit went…

"Eurggggg," said Georgie, pulling himself up the stonework and lurching onto the roof.

“I’m surprised the Shadowmongers haven’t got either of you yet,” Hilda called as they came to stand on either side of Mummy. “That will be corrected shortly! So,” she continued in a business-like tone, “it’s what, three against a hundred?”

“Make it five,” growled Marty, clawing his way onto the roof, a furious-looking Wilhelmina clinging to his back.

“You mean ten,” corrected a suit of armour, appearing beside the werewolf – a suit of armour

with a long, jagged crack running the length of his breastplate. Four more suits popped up beside him, making quite a racket as they scaled the wall of the mansion.

"Twelve," chorused Bob and Sally, the gargoyles, landing beside the MLM in a crunch of stone.

"Fine: *twelve* against a hundred," Hilda conceded. "Now, before we obliterate you, I think some introductions are in order: members of the once-mighty MLM, meet the MSM!"

Wilhelmina frowned. "The MSM?"

"The Monster Squad of Monsters, of course! With a stated mission to—"

"We know, WE KNOW!" she retorted.

"What a dumb name," scoffed Marty.

Hilda shrugged. "My co-founder, the late Abrax, chose it. Personally, I wanted something with a bit more *oomph*, but it was a small concession on my part. It's a shame he can't be here today," she added, gaze sliding to Mummy, who'd defeated Abrax at Halloween.

"Enough talk," said Miles, sliding off the back of the skele-crow.

"Quite right," Hilda agreed.

The crocoman began shouting out orders, which the monsters of the MSM hastened to follow. Wilhelmina turned to the MLM, eyeing each member in turn. "Good luck and devil-speed," she said. And with that, the once-powerful witch crossed the roof to stand beside Theodora.

"Lost your touch, Wilhelmina?" called one witch.

"Might as well be human!" cackled another.

"They're not going to try to fight the MSM – are they?" Theodora asked Wilhelmina.

"You can't expect them to just stand aside and let Hilda take over, can you?"

"No," Theodora replied in a small voice, shoulders sagging. How would the MLM ever survive this? Sure, she'd seen them accomplish seemingly impossible feats before, but *this*?

"Attaaaaacck!" bellowed Miles.

At the crocoman's command, the MSM charged, their collective footsteps so punishing they caused the roof tiles to shake beneath Theodora's trainers.

"How do you want to handle this, Mummy?" asked

Marty, surveying the incoming army.

"The way we always do: together."

The werewolf nodded.

Mummy looked over to where the children stood, seeking not Theodora or Sherman, or even Wilhelmina, but Althea. "Take care of Theodora," she said, taking her place at the helm of the MLM. "On my count," she began, nodding to the monsters on either side of her.

"One."

Marty dropped into a crouch, extending his claws. Bandit bared his fangs and Georgie (rather grotesquely) distended his jaw.

"Two," Mummy called, lifting her knives as the suits of armour unsheathed their swords and the gargoyles flexed their great, stone wings.

"Three!"

And with that, the Battle of Thirteen Battington Lane began.

The Battle of Thirteen Battington Lane

Now, before we go any further, I must impress upon you the importance of this event: this was no mere struggle for power, no mean fight for glory. This was a battle for the very soul of monsterdom: should Hilda and the MSM emerge victorious, humans everywhere would be in terrible peril. If there was no more MLM, no more Headquarters, no more rules, who would stop bad vampires from draining people of their blood? Who would prevent wicked werewolves from attacking couples out for a moonlit stroll? Who would thwart enterprising hags from snatching children from their beds? You can see, I'm sure, how much was at stake.

And so, to the battle.

Marty was the first to attack, launching himself at

the werewolves. Mummy was hot on his paws, felling any monster foolish enough to cross her path. Bob and Sally flew at the witches, snapping their wands in half while the knights circled Miles, dodging his vicious, snapping jaws and blocking his razor-sharp claws with their swords. Georgie swallowed the demons whole, spitting out their spears like toothpicks while Bandit darted between the hobgoblins, biting and clawing with a ferocity usually reserved for hunting vampire-mice.

Speaking of which, did you know that a group of mice is called a "mischief"? What's that – you're wondering why I'm giving you a vocabulary lesson at a time like this? Well, it's because at that very moment, a horde of vampire-mice were streaming onto the roof via a drainage pipe, intending to cause their own brand of, ahem, *mischief*.

The vampire-mice swarmed the members of the MSM, nibbling on the unsuspecting monsters' ankles and knocking them off balance. Soon, their efforts were doubled as the vampire-mice were joined by some other Masters of Mischief: the werewolf cubs. With Sylvester taking the lead, the pups waded into the melee, biting the MSM's calves and knees.

Theodora watched the scene unfold with eyes as round as dinner plates. Her monsters were holding their own, but for how long? More of the MSM were watching from the sidelines – a quick tally counted fifty of them – fresh and fit and waiting to enter the fray at Miles' command. Not to mention the Shadowmongers, which seemed to have disappeared for the moment but were undoubtedly near by…

"There must be something we can do to help!" she cried as a knight's helmet soared past her head.

"We can help by getting out of here," said Althea.

"You're right," Wilhelmina agreed. "The MLM

don't need the added pressure of worrying about our safety."

"I'm not leaving Mummy," Theodora said stoutly, pulling out the pouch Wilhelmina had given her at the Monster UN. Maybe it held something that could help. She couldn't – no, wouldn't – abandon her family: not now, not ever. She removed its meagre contents: the Sight Extender and the photograph.

"Watch out!" Althea cried, pushing Theodora down as something whooshed over their heads. The *something* was a spell – a powerful one, judging by the way it caused her hair to stand on end as it passed.

"There's more where that came from!" called a witch, sending another spell on its tail.

"No!" Dexter cried, grabbing the Sight Extender out of Theodora's hands and bravely leaping in front of his friends. He raised the instrument before him like a shield. This time, the bright blue eyeball blinked. The spell bounced off the lens, rebounding upon its caster. The witch fell to the floor, motionless. Another hurried to take her place, hurling curse after curse their way, each of which Dexter deftly deflected with the Sight Extender. ("You could play pro-tennis!" Sherman cried, cheering him on.)

“We’ve got to move,” Wilhelmina shouted over the din of the battle. “There!” she said, pointing to a door set in the roof.

“Where will you go?” Mummy yelled as they scurried past, a spray of sickly orange blood arcing through the air as she cleanly separated a hobgoblin’s head from its body.

“The graveyard – Figaro and the ghosts will protect us!” Wilhelmina replied, pulling at the door, which swung open to reveal none other than … a Shadowmonger. A massive Shadowmonger. It was one of the bears, swiping its oversized paws through the air, missing Dexter by mere centimetres.

"Get back!" Theodora cried, as not one but several of the shadowy creatures eked onto the roof like smoky black clouds. "It's the Shadowmongers!"

"Finally!" Hilda roared, raising her staff in triumph. "Let's start with the cat and the zombie, shall we?" she asked, a truly wicked gleam creeping into her eyes.

The MSM melted away, leaving Georgie and Bandit quite alone. The Shadowmongers descended upon them like a cloud of gnats, and before Theodora could do more than shout "Watch out!" a pair of horses galloped through the two friends.

"No!" Theodora screeched, watching in dismay as the Shadowmongers' magic took effect: Bandit was shrinking, his eyes growing rounder, his fur growing fluffier, until a mewling kitten stood in place of the formerly fierce feline. At the same time, Georgie began to shrink and shrivel, the scent of burnt rubbish filling Theodora's nostrils as he withered. Within seconds, the zombie had been reduced to a pile of dust.

"Georgie," Sherman moaned.

"Someone h-help Bandit,"

Dexter barked, blocking another curse with the Sight Extender. "He's g-gonna g-get trampled!"

"I'll get him," said Althea, darting forward. She zigged and zagged, dodging both the spells and the fighting. She plucked the kitten off the roof and not a moment too soon, for in the next instant a hobgoblin's axe sliced through the roof tile upon which he had sat. But Theodora did not see what happened next; something else had caught her attention … the shadow monkey, hopping along the air currents, eyes pinned on Mummy. Mummy, of course, couldn't see him, and before Theodora could call out, the Shadowmonger had leapt through Mummy's shoulder.

Time seemed to slow. Theodora's breath caught in her throat as Mummy gasped, falling in a graceful arc. Her arms came to rest across her chest, her faithful knives still clutched in her hands. Her eyes fluttered shut as if she'd been laid to rest; all that was missing was her sarcophagus. Vaguely, Theodora heard the sound of someone screaming. It was a full minute before she realized the someone was her.

"Theodora, come!" Althea ordered, half-dragging her towards the door, away from the battle, away from Mummy. Theodora pulled away, but Althea said, "Mummy wouldn't want you to give up – she'd want you to try to help your friends!"

Her words acted like a balm of sorts. Theodora's screams died on her lips; her tears stilled on her cheeks. Althea was right – Mummy wouldn't want her to give up. And though it was one of the hardest things she would ever do, Theodora turned away from Mummy, following Althea to where Dexter, Sherman and a pale-faced Wilhelmina were waiting.

"Get help!" Marty yelled as they scrambled past. "I don't know how much longer we can keep this up!"

No sooner had he spoken than a tall, thin figure landed upon the roof, silent as a shadow. A figure with oil-slick hair and skin paler than the moon: Dracula, of course.

"You're not to join in any fighting directly," Wilhelmina said at once. "You're an Agency Head; it's against policy!"

"What kind of leader would I be if I didn't help my team when they needed me most?" he countered. "Theodora, Dexter, Sherman, I'm going to fly you three down to the garden. I'll come back for you, Wilhelmina, and you, Human-I've-Never-Met," he added to Althea. "Then I'll join the battle. Now, is anyone hurt?"

"A few of the knights have lost their heads – I mean, helmets," Dexter supplied. "And the Shadowmongers got Georgie, Bandit and Mummy—"

"They got *Mummy*?" yelped the vampire.

It happened very suddenly: Dracula's lips twisted into a snarl, his fangs lengthened, his nostrils flared. But it was the change in his eyes that was most alarming: they went flat, empty – like a shark's. Theodora felt, rather than saw, the others shudder, drawing close to one another as if this would protect them from the terrifying creature standing before them. Only Theodora seemed unperturbed by

Dracula's transformation – but then, she'd seen such a change occur in him once before.

Instantly forgetting his offer to fly the others down to safety, Dracula waded into battle. Sensing the predator among them, the MSM shrank back – not that this would save them. Mummy may have been regarded as the world's greatest warrior, but, as Theodora watched the vampire's progress, she couldn't help thinking that he was just as worthy of the title. Within minutes he had obliterated most of the remaining monsters, sinking his fangs into their necks and—

You know what? I don't think I'll describe the rest; it's much too gruesome, and if I *do* I'm afraid that you'll have nightmares and then your parents might forbid you from finishing this book and we are so very close to the end. Let's just say it wasn't a pretty sight.

"Get him!" Hilda screamed at her army of Shadowmongers. "Get them all!"

The creatures swooped down, surrounding Dracula like a shadowy whirlpool. Another group of them circled Bob and Sally while a third rounded up the knights and a fourth corralled the vampire-mice and the werewolf cubs.

Theodora watched the creatures descend, transfixed. This was it, she knew it: the end of the MLM. Dracula seemed to know it too: he kneeled beside Mummy, taking her too-still hand into his own. A small sob escaped Theodora's throat – they'd never even got to go on their date…

But before the Shadowmongers could strike, a sound like an explosion rocked the roof – probably because it *was* an explosion. Theodora looked around to locate the source. It had come from the chimney – *Goldie's* chimney.

The Shadow Catcher

The wosnak's gilded head burst through the chimney, raining brick and plaster onto the heads of those nearest to her.

"You're not dead!" Sherman said, ecstatic.

"I wasssss asssssleep. Lasssssst time I have warrrrrrrm milk beforrrrre bedddddd."

An awestruck Miles stared at Goldie, transfixed. "It's true, then?" the crocoman asked. "A wosnak actually lives here?"

"What's the big deal?" scoffed an MSM demon.

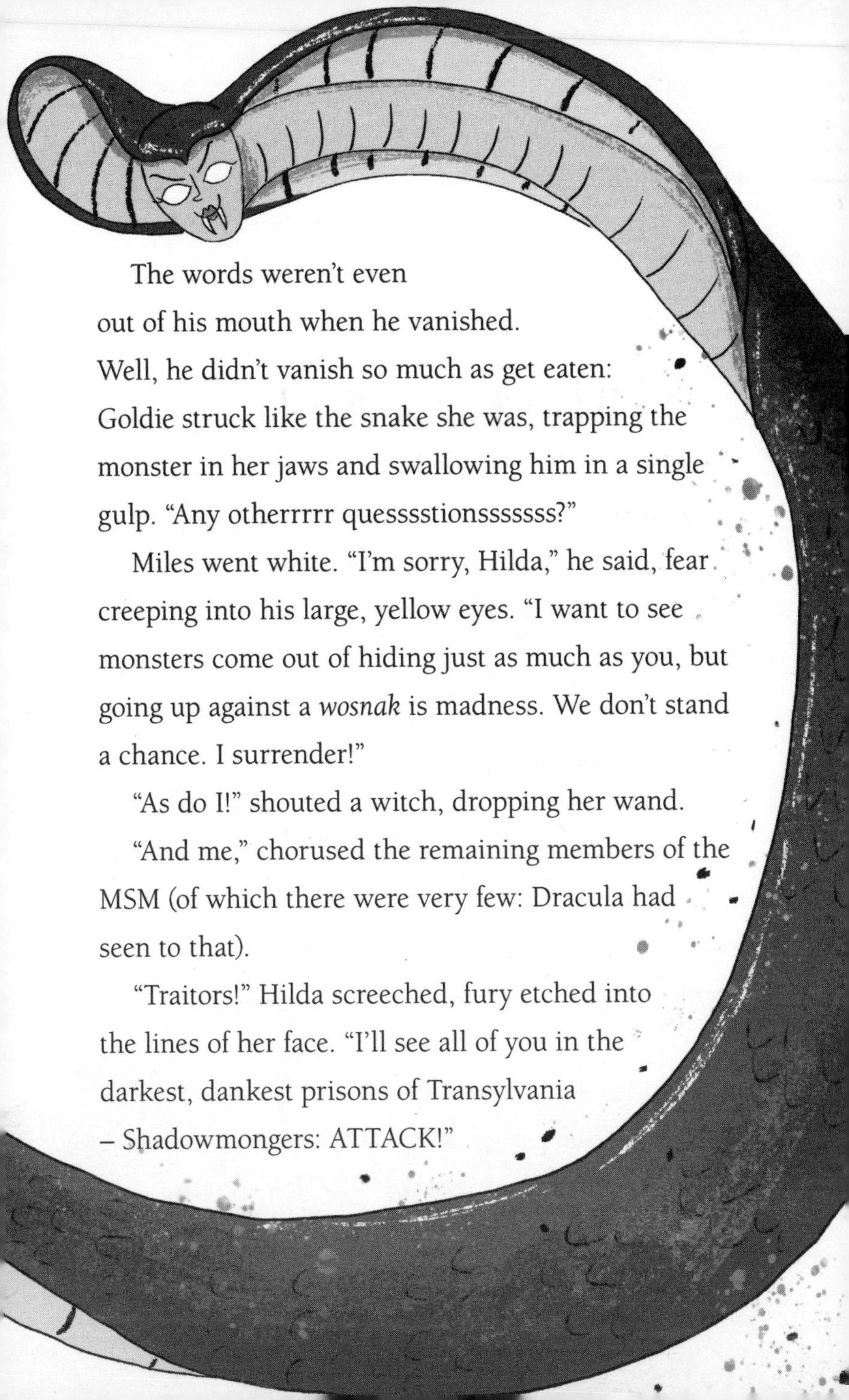

The words weren't even out of his mouth when he vanished. Well, he didn't vanish so much as get eaten: Goldie struck like the snake she was, trapping the monster in her jaws and swallowing him in a single gulp. "Any otherrrrr quesssstionsssssss?"

Miles went white. "I'm sorry, Hilda," he said, fear creeping into his large, yellow eyes. "I want to see monsters come out of hiding just as much as you, but going up against a *wosnak* is madness. We don't stand a chance. I surrender!"

"As do I!" shouted a witch, dropping her wand.

"And me," chorused the remaining members of the MSM (of which there were very few: Dracula had seen to that).

"Traitors!" Hilda screeched, fury etched into the lines of her face. "I'll see all of you in the darkest, dankest prisons of Transylvania – Shadowmongers: ATTACK!"

The animals swarmed, circling the remaining monsters, MLM and MSM alike. Goldie, though she could not see them, blew short, sharp bursts of fire in their direction. Theodora, who of course *could* see them, watched as the creatures reared back; they clearly did not like the heat – or perhaps it was the light that offended them so. Still, it was only a matter of time before Goldie would tire, or miss one, before one of the beasts slipped through her defences…

There had to be something Theodora could do. She was sure she was missing something, but what? And then it hit her like a ton of cauldrons.

When she'd asked Goldie for a way to defeat the Shadowmongers, the wosnak had shown her a mirror – which was useless, as far as she and Sherman had been concerned. But what if they'd misunderstood? What if the mirror itself wasn't the answer, but rather what it represented? After all, the whole point of having a mirror was to see your reflection. Did that mean – could it be? – that she, Theodora, was the key to stopping the Shadowmongers?

And if so, the real question was, *how*? How would she, a human – and a kid at that – be able to stop creatures so terrible that even monsters as ferocious as Mummy and Dracula were unable to defeat them? There was nothing special about her: she had no great strengths, no magical powers, no anything. Or did she?

"Maybe the reason the Shadowmongers can't be defeated by monsters is because they don't have the right skills," she said slowly, turning to Dexter. "But maybe humans do..."

"H-humans who know how to build a Shadow Catcher," he suggested, meeting her gaze.

"Exactly. The only problem is, it's back in my room..."

Dexter smiled. "No, it's not," he said, pulling the Shadow Catcher out of his satchel. "W-what were the odds that we would b-be b-building a *Shadow Catcher* at the exact same time the mansion was under attack b-by *Shadowmongers*? I f-figured it couldn't just be a c-coincidence, so I grabbed it on the w-way out. Here," he continued, passing the Shadow Catcher to Theodora. The cardboard was slightly crushed, and some of their painted-on designs had smudged, but it was very much intact.

"I'm sure you did a good job," Althea said kindly, "but I don't think a Year Five science project will defeat supernatural beings."

But Wilhelmina had a different perspective. "I'm with Dexter: there are no coincidences. And from what I've seen, the universe has a strange way of evening itself out..."

"'Every action has an equal and opposite reaction,'" Theodora quoted, parroting Ms Frumple's words.

"Precisely. I—" Wilhelmina cut off as a loud, scraping sound tore through the night. Theodora turned towards the noise. It seemed the Shadowmongers had finally broken through Goldie's defences, turning two more monsters, Bob and Sally, into lifeless chunks of stone.

Galvanized by this sad, sorry sight, Theodora pulled at Dexter's sleeve. "Let's go," she said.

"W-wait," he said, pulling away. "W-we should put it over there instead." He pointed further along the roof.

"But..."

"Theodora, do you k-know why I'm g-good at chess? It's cos I've g-got a knack for predicting my o-opponent's next step. I have a feeling about this. Trust m-me, OK?"

And though Theodora was worried that they were making a mistake, one look at her friend's earnest face convinced her otherwise; if she couldn't trust Dexter after all that they had been through, then she couldn't trust anyone. She nodded, and together they crossed the roof, coming to a stop in front of the very turret upon which Mummy had stood. Carefully, they arranged the Shadow Catcher upon it, in the full light of the moon. Testing its position, Dexter placed a hand behind the parchment, blocking the moonlight. A hand-shaped shadow appeared.

"If this w-works the w-way I think it should, when the Shadow-m-mongers f-fly in f-front of the moon, their shadow should get caught in the b-box, so to speak," Dexter explained. "We just have to h-hope that their sh-shadows, unlike ours, s-stay there…"

Theodora nodded in reply. She was staring at the pouch's last item, the photograph. She gazed at it for a moment more, then carefully placed it at the front of the Shadow Catcher, in the exact spot where the creatures' shadows would hopefully appear.

"We should get away from here, lest Hilda catch us," Sherman said.

But it was too late: the hag had spotted them. "And

just what do you think you're doing?" she croaked.

"Defeating your Shadowmongers, once and for all!" Theodora said bravely.

"With a child's toy?" Hilda guffawed.

"If you're so sure it won't work, why don't you summon the Shadowmongers?"

"With pleasure," hissed the hag.

And just as Dexter had predicted they would, the Shadowmongers flew towards them, moving as one. They soared past the moon, directly into the Shadow Catcher's path. Theodora held her breath, willing

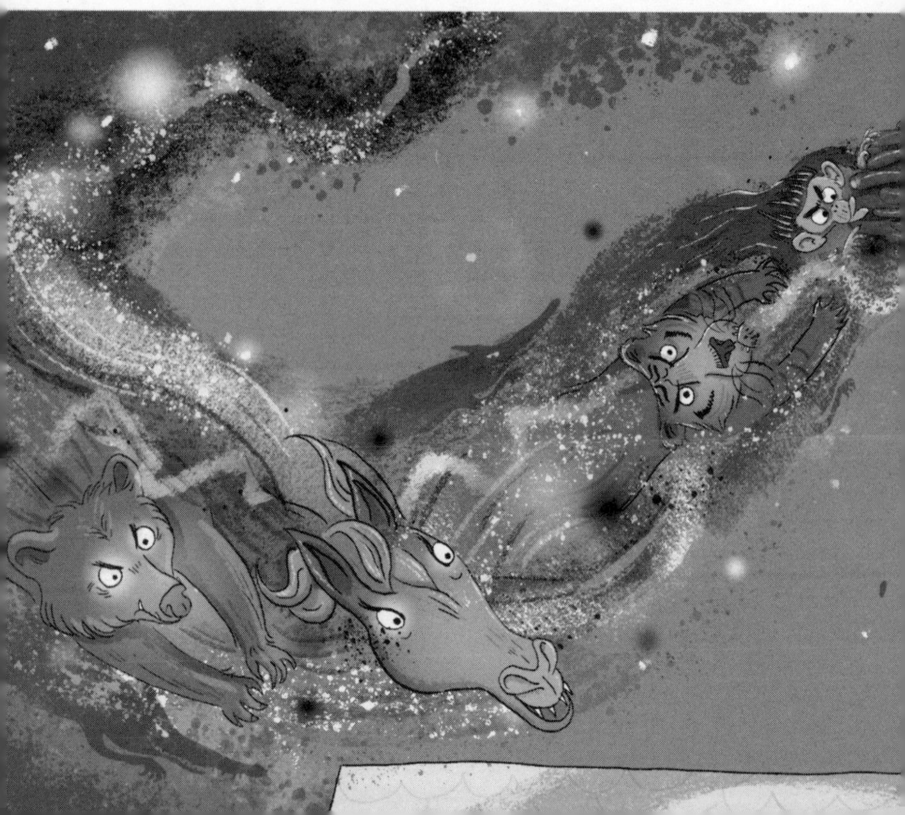

their plan to work. At first, nothing happened, but then something astonishing – no, astounding – no, amazing – transpired: one by one, the beasts' shadows darkened the parchment paper of the Shadow Catcher. And one by one, the beasts were vanishing, disintegrating in the moonlight as if all that had tethered them to the earth was, alas, their shadows.

"W-what's happening?" Dexter whispered, catching sight of Theodora's shining face.

"We did it – the Shadowmongers have gone!"

A furious scream tore from Hilda's throat. "This is your fault!" she raged, banging her staff against the roof. A sword shot out of its tip, zooming towards Theodora, who didn't have time to blink, let alone move out of the way. But a knight – one with a long, jagged crack running the length of his breastplate – threw his own sword through the air with deadly accuracy, forcing the blade off course.

Undeterred, Hilda banged her walking stick again. This time, a large fishing net erupted from it. It whipped through the air, heading for Theodora. But Hilda was stymied once more: Marty leapt in front of Theodora just as the net fell.

"Not on my watch!" he cried, biting through the mesh.

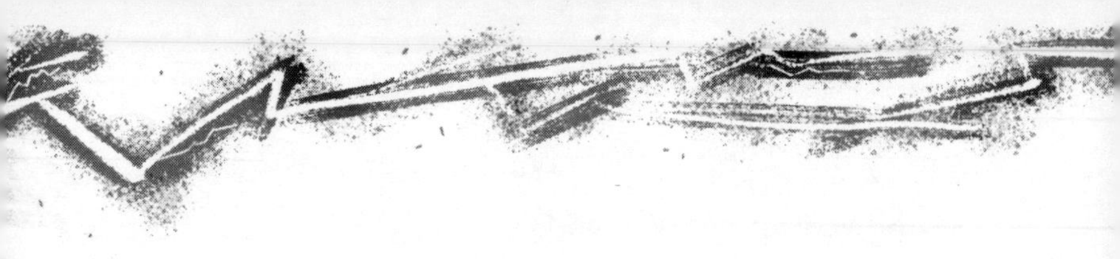

With a snarl, Hilda swirled her walking stick above her head, as if she were trying to lasso the stars. And perhaps she had, for a ray so white and bright it might have been made of starlight shot at Theodora. This time, it was Dracula who took the force of Hilda's wrath, the beam striking him in the exact place where his un-beating heart sat in his chest. Theodora's own heart was thrumming as quickly as a hummingbird's – she couldn't lose Dracula, too – but to her surprise, the ray had no effect on the vampire.

"The stars are part of the night," he said softly, "and so am I."

"Enough," hissed Goldie, eyes blazing. She took a deep, shuddering breath, steeling herself for one last strike. She exhaled, a ring of fire encircling Hilda. But the hag was ready for her, squeezing her heels against the skele-crow's sides before the flames could trap them. The fowl took flight, rising up into the air.

Dracula made to give chase, but Wilhelmina stopped him. "It's no use," she said.

And she was right: the skele-crow was growing smaller by the second, a speck against the giant, silvery orb that was the moon. And then it was gone, swallowed up by the clouds.

"Members of the army formally known as the MSM," Dracula said in a commanding voice, "you are hereby under arrest!"

"What members?" asked Wilhelmina. "The Shadowmongers got them all."

"They got most of us, too," Marty said sadly.

"I'm sure Headquarters is very close to figuring out a way to reverse the Shadowmongers' curse," Wilhelmina said briskly.

"I wouldn'tttttt bettttt on ittttt," hissed Goldie. "Only a wossssssnak can reverssssse the Ssssshadowmongerssss effectttts."

"Ahhhhh." Sherman sighed. "We asked Goldie how to stop the Shadowmongers but didn't think to ask her how to reverse their effects. A rookie mistake!"

"Can you help us, Goldie?" Theodora asked, something very much like hope blossoming in her chest. "Do you want us to answer a riddle? Or give you a gift?"

Goldie tilted her head, considering. "Nooooo. I have alrrrrready recccccеived one."

"What's that?"

"Youuuuu." And with that, Goldie exhaled one last time, flames shooting from her jaws. Droplets of fire dripped from the blaze, falling to the roof like rain. The little flames sprouted arms and legs, standing to attention as they awaited the wosnak's instructions.

"What are those?" asked Sherman, squinting at them through his cracked monocles.

"Liggggggght bearerssssss."

The Light Bearers

"And they can reverse the effects of the Shadow-mongers?" asked Dracula, hardly daring to hope.

In reply, Goldie nodded at the nearest blaze. The little flame took off, moving at the speed of light. (See what I did there?) It raced towards Mummy's still form, running up her leg and across her shoulder before settling on her head. After a beat, the flame flickered, then died. Mummy's eyes popped open. Her arms uncrossed as she rose to a sitting position. She sheathed her knives, then stood, blinking rapidly.

Theodora ran towards her, throwing her arms around Mummy's waist. "You're alive!" she cried.

"Theodora, you're crushing me," wheezed Mummy, laughing.

"Sorry," she sniffled. "I thought you were..."

“There, there,” Mummy said, kissing her forehead. “Everything’s OK now.”

“Almosssssst,” Goldie quipped. “Lighttt bearersssss, onwarrrrrds.”

The tiny blazes, now numbering in the hundreds, set off in all directions: some ran right over the edge of the roof and down the sides of the house, disappearing into the grounds, racing over mountains and crossing oceans in search of those injured by the Shadowmongers. Others leapt down the chimney, speeding through the corridors of the mansion. Others still remained on the rooftop, reviving the members of the MLM and the MSM alike, who one by one returned to their monster forms.

Finally, there was only one flame left. Gently disentangling herself from Mummy's embrace, Theodora stepped towards it. As it had with the others, the blaze raced up her frame and settled on her head. And just like that, the chill she'd felt since the shadow lions had struck her vanished. Warmth flooded through her body as if she'd slipped into a steaming hot bath, along with a feeling of great relief: that night, for the first time in over a month, her sleep would not be haunted by nightmares.

"Theodora…?" Mummy asked.

"The Shadowmongers got me when we escaped from the UN," she admitted. "I didn't tell you because, well, there was nothing you could do. I didn't want you to worry."

"Oh, Theodora, it's not your job to worry about me!" Mummy chided gently.

"I know," Theodora said.

"We're going to talk about this later."

"I know that, too."

"How can we ever thank you, Goldie?" asked Wilhelmina.

"You cannnnn't," the wosnak replied, a rare smile gracing her face as she slithered back into her tower.

"We should head in too," said Dracula. "Bob, Sally,

would you please take our prisoners to the dungeons? I'm sure Headquarters will be most interested in hearing about what they've been up to..."

While the gargoyles dealt with what remained of the MSM, everyone else made their way back into the mansion. It still bore signs of the recent battle, but never mind that now: for there, standing in the foyer, was Helter-Skelter.

"Can I get anyone a snack, or a monstertail – or perhaps a bath?" asked the butler, grinning from ear to ear (or at least, he would have been, if he still had lips).

"You're back!" Theodora cried, giving him a hug.

"I am," he said. "And – oh, hello," Helter-Skelter added, catching sight of Althea. "Er, is everyone aware that there's another human in the mansion?"

As one, the monsters, Theodora and Dexter looked at Althea. Theodora had nearly forgotten about her – she'd been so quiet while the light bearers did their work.

"Of course," said Dracula. "Erm, who are you?"

"My name is Althea."

"She came out of Theodora's torat pack," Sherman volunteered. "She was trapped inside *The Lady* card, then moved to *The Empress*, which she broke free of when it caught fire and—"

"But who *are* you?" Dracula asked her.

"I think I know," said Theodora, finally ready to voice the thought that had begun taking shape in her mind the instant Althea's grass-green gaze had met her own. "You're my…" She hesitated, eyes darting nervously to Mummy, who nodded for her to continue. "You're my – well, you're my human mother."

"I am," Althea agreed, her eyes shining brightly.

The monsters let out a collective gasp. Only Mummy did not seem surprised, though her smile had become rather fixed. Theodora felt as if the very ground had shifted beneath her feet. It was one thing to suspect that she had found her human mother; it was quite another to know it.

"I owe you all an explanation," Althea said.

"Especially you, Theodora."

"Perhaps we should sit down," Dracula suggested, leading the way to the Beelzebub Parlour – it, at least, had escaped the battle unscathed. Once they were seated, Althea began.

"It all started ten years ago. We – your father and I – had just moved to Appleton. I was at the farmers' market looking to purchase some Halloween pumpkins when I noticed that the man selling them wasn't *actually* a man: he had a pumpkin for a head. I screamed, then ran all the way home. Now I know that he was – is – Sir Pumpkin-de-Patch."

"Did someone say my name?" asked the Monster-Gardener-in-Chief, walking into the room accompanied by a grinning Marty. Grimeny Cricket hopped in behind them, along with the rest of the MLM, including the trolls and the librarians, Mousetrap clutching Hamlet in his talons. Even the vampire-mice wanted to join the reunion, poking their heads out of their mouseholes (and poking them right back in when they caught sight of Bandit, eyeing them with interest). Cheers were cheered, hugs were hugged, kisses were kissed. Finally, everyone settled, and Althea picked up the thread of her tale once more.

"A week later I saw you, Wilhelmina, amongst others – including Hilda – and then I knew: there were monsters in Appleton. And I seemed to be the only one who could see them."

At this, Mummy, Wilhelmina and Dracula exchanged startled looks.

"My husband didn't believe me – not at first," Althea continued. "Six months passed, and by then our family of two had become three. You were just one month old, Theodora, when there was a knock at the door. I opened it to find a monster standing on the

other side. He said he was a representative of Headquarters—"

"You're sure he said Headquarters?" Dracula interrupted.

A shadow moved behind Althea's eyes. "Oh, yes. He said that because I could see through glamours – at the time, I had no idea what that meant – I was a risk to the MLM Charter. He tried to force me to leave with him… We fought and he left."

"How on earth did you manage that?" Wilhelmina asked in amazement.

"I hit him on the head with a frying pan," Althea said ruefully. "But the next week he returned, and the week after that, and the week after *that*… We decided to go away, first to Majorca, then to Argentina – we even went to Alaska! – but he always found us. We realized, then, that I needed to go into hiding. But where?"

"The torat cards," Sherman whispered, all eight of his eyes unblinking, in rapt attention.

"One day, I bumped into this woman. I recognized her right away – well, she's a rather famous magazine editor. She said she knew of my troubles and offered me her assistance."

"Eurg," said Georgie knowingly.

"Yes, she was – is – the leader of the rata-tat-tats."

"Meow? Mew!" said Bandit, which probably meant, "Really? Rata-tat-tats aren't known for their generosity – they're rude and stuck-up and I don't like them at all, not one little bit!"

Althea shrugged. "Even so, she put me into the torat pack, promising that I would be able to break free when the time was right – when you needed me most, Theodora."

"So, you were gone," Theodora pressed, determined to get the whole story. "And then my human father left me in a graveyard. Why?"

"By then he knew too much. He was afraid of what Headquarters might do to him – let alone to you – if they found out."

"So, he abandoned me?"

"He would never abandon you!"

"Well, what would *you* call leaving someone in a graveyard?" Theodora demanded hotly.

"He didn't! I mean, yes, he left you in the graveyard," she allowed. "But he knew Georgie would be waking up from his nap – he knew you'd be found by the MLM."

"I knew it," said Mummy, a triumphant gleam in her eyes. "I *knew* that whoever left Theodora in the graveyard meant for her to be ours!"

"Hold on," Theodora interrupted. "He meant for me to be found by monsters? But why? I mean, I'm glad and all, but that's sort of—"

"W-weird." Dexter nodded.

"Well, who better to protect you than the MLM? We feared you had inherited my ability to see through glamours – rightly so, I might add – and that Headquarters would one day come for you, too."

"Seems l-like a l-lot of people can," Dexter mused. "See through glamours, I mean."

Mummy, Dracula and Wilhelmina exchanged another look. But before they could ask Dexter what he meant, there was a ktnock at the door.

All's Well That Ends Well

"That m-must be my m-mom," said Dexter, jumping to his feet.

"Hurry," urged Mummy.

Dexter scurried from the room. "Hi, Mom," they heard him say from the hallway.

No reply was forthcoming. Instead, the distinctive sound of heels clicking against wood filled their ears. An instant later, Mrs Adebola appeared in the parlour. Her gaze widened at the sight of the battle-worn monsters. For a moment, nobody spoke. And then: "What on earth happened here?" she demanded. "The front garden is covered in rubbish – I found this," she said, tossing a broken brick onto the rug, "on the path and this," she added, tossing a chicken-sized talon beside it, "on your doorstep. The hallway looks like it's been ransacked, and—"

"If you think the hallway's bad," Sherman said drily, "you ought to see the roof."

"Not in front of the human," Wilhelmina hissed.

"It's OK," Theodora assured her. "She already knows that you're monsters; she can see through glamours. Right, Mrs Adebola?"

And Mrs Adebola finally admitted that this was true. "Right," she agreed.

"But *three* humans who can see through glamours?"

"Four, if you count my Aunt Dede," Dexter said.

"Will someone please fill me in?" Mrs Adebola said.

"Sit down," suggested Mummy. "We'll explain."

"That is … a lot of information to receive in thirty minutes," Mrs Adebola said when they'd finished. "I can't believe you fought off witches," she added, staring at her son in amazement.

"Dexter did very well." Wilhelmina smiled. "Can you tell us more about this ability of yours to see through glamours?"

Before Mrs Adebola could reply, there was another knock at the door. "I'll get it," she offered, rising to her feet. But it was too late: Mrs Next Door, Mrs Across the Street and Mr Down the Road had apparently let themselves in, and the three of them now came striding into the parlour.

"Now see here," Mrs Next Door began. "We've put up with your house being in disrepair; we've put up with your garish decorations; we've put up with your comings and goings at all hours of the day and night, but we draw the line at all that gosh-darn racket you've been making..." She trailed off, only then seeming to notice that she was standing in a room full of monsters. "Oh, my," she breathed, taking a step back.

"Well, I'll be damned," said Mr Down the Road, as Figaro, Pimms and the rest of the ghosts floated in through the wall. "They *do* exist."

Mrs Across the Street promptly fainted.

"Erm," Dracula began, shifting uncomfortably. "I can explain—"

"Allow me," said Wilhelmina, withdrawing her wand from her cloak. There was a sound like a balloon popping, and then all three neighbours were on the floor, asleep. Another pop, and the trio vanished. "They'll wake up in their own beds tomorrow morning, thinking this was all just some bizarre dream," Wilhelmina said, looking rather pleased with herself.

Mrs Adebola rose to her feet. "We should go too. I'm sure you all have a lot to talk about," she said, glancing at Althea, Theodora and Mummy.

"We wanted to ask you more about your ability to see through glamours," Dracula said quickly. "Perhaps you could join us for tea next week?"

Mrs Adebola flashed him a white, toothy grin. "Certainly."

"Will you be OK?" Dexter whispered to Theodora as he gathered his things.

"Sure," Theodora said, though she couldn't look him in the eye. It was all so much to take in, and in truth, she didn't know if things *would* be OK.

They waved goodbye, leaving Theodora, Althea and the monsters alone once more.

"Well, I suppose there's just one thing left to discuss," Mummy said, turning to Theodora.

"I imagine you'll want to live with Althea, now that you've found each other."

"Mew!" said Bandit, which probably meant, "But Theodora can't leave!"

"Awooooo," Sylvester howled in agreement.

Theodora's gaze darted between Mummy and Althea. "I – I," she began, licking her lips. But what was there to say? If she were being honest, she *did* want to get to know Althea – of course she did. But then, Theodora thought guiltily, what about Mummy? What about Dracula and Wilhelmina and Georgie and Bandit and—

"Naturally, Theodora wants to stay here, with her family," Althea said.

"You're her family too."

"True," she agreed. "And I've missed out on so much, having spent most of Theodora's life trapped in the torat pack… Which is why I was hoping I might be able to stay here too," she said quietly, looking at Mummy now.

"But what about the Rules?" challenged Grimeny Cricket.

"Stuff the Rules, I say," said Wilhelmina. "Besides, Headquarters isn't exactly following them if they're hunting down humans who can see through glamours, are they?"

"I do think we need to do something about that," Grimeny Cricket acknowledged, hopping away in search of his quill. (I have a hunch we'll be seeing another brief from him soon.)

"We certainly don't want Headquarters going after Althea again," said Pimms.

"No, we don't," agreed Marty. "And we can protect her better if she's here."

"True," said Sir Pumpkin-de-Patch. "We'll just have to keep her presence a secret."

"Luckily, we've got *plenty* of experience with that," Bon said with a wink at Theodora.

"Would you like that, Theodora?" asked Mummy. "Would you like to continue living here with us – and Althea?"

"Very much," said Theodora, slipping her hand into Mummy's.

"Thennnnn that's settttttttttttttled," sang Figaro, clapping his ghostly hands in delight.

"I think a party is in order," said Helter-Skelter, bustling into the parlour with an armful of decorations. "Althea, welcome to the family!" This was greeted by howls and cheers. Within a half hour, they had strung streamers around the room, Helter-Skelter had whipped up a delectable platter of goodies, and everyone was enjoying a nice, well-deserved monstertail. Yes, it looked like they were in for an excellent celebration indeed.

"Althea," said Dracula, "perhaps you and Theodora might like to go to dinner next weekend? Mummy and I are due a date," he said, holding out his hand to Mummy, which she graciously accepted. As he did, something fluttered to the floor without him noticing – an old, crumpled business card.

"I would like that," Althea said, beaming at Theodora.

"Me too." Theodora smiled at Althea. "I just have one last question – for now. What happened to my human dad? He's not trapped in my torat pack too, is he? Probably not," she added as an afterthought. "He must be somewhere far, far away if he managed to stay off Headquarters' radar all this time..."

Althea plucked the fallen card from the carpet, smoothing the wrinkled paper. "Oh, he might not have gone as far as you think," she said cryptically, brushing her fingers against the lopsided eye of the logo. "Now, if you don't mind, I'd like to change out of these robes."

"I have something you can borrow," Mummy offered.

"Thank you." Althea flashed Theodora a mysterious smile, passing her the business card as she followed Mummy out of the parlour.

"Her explanation about your human father was about as clear as mud – she could give Goldie a run for her money," Sherman said. "I wonder what she meant?"

"So do I," Theodora said, slipping the card into her pocket. "But I'm sure we'll find out, one way or another."

"We always do," he agreed. "Now, shall we join the party?"

"Definitely!"

I'm sure you'll be pleased to hear that we have just one last loose end to tie up – a big, Frumple-shaped loose end. (You didn't forget about *her*, did you?)

The Invitation

The following Monday, Theodora arrived at school early. She headed straight to Ms Frumple's office and knocked on the door.

"Come in."

Theodora straightened her hair ribbon, squared her shoulders and entered the office.

"Good morning, Ms Frumple," she said, dropping into her usual chair.

"To what do I owe this *pleasure*?" asked the head teacher, with a frown of *dis*pleasure.

"I wanted to hand in my science project," Theodora replied, unzipping her knapsack and placing the Shadow Catcher (looking distinctly worse for wear) on the desk.

Ms Frumple eyed it warily. "Did you test it to ensure that it works?"

"Oh, yeah." Theodora grinned, recalling the Battle of Thirteen Battington Lane. "It definitely works."

"Hm. We'll see. You may return to class now, Ms Hendrix."

"I also wanted to hand in my family tree assignment," Theodora said, holding out a small posterboard.

Ms Frumple didn't move to take it. "This was due over a month ago," she said. "I'm afraid I can't accept it."

"But that's not fair!" Theodora cried, outraged. "I worked really hard on this! Ask my mum, if you don't believe me."

"Oh, I shall," said Ms Frumple, picking up the phone. "There's much I need to discuss with her."

"No need to dial," said a voice. "I'm right here."

There, standing in the doorway, was Althea. She was no longer dressed in the pale blue robes she'd worn in *The Lady* – and later *The Empress* – card, but a neat little dress that Mummy had lent her. "May I?" she asked, stepping into the office.

Ms Frumple's pale gaze roved over Althea, lingering on her eyes. "Who are you?" she asked rather rudely.

"Theodora's mum," Althea replied, coming to stand beside Theodora.

"Please," Ms Frumple scoffed. "I've met Theodora's

mum on more occasions than I care to count, and you're not her."

"You've met my mummy," Theodora corrected. "This is my *mum*."

Ms Frumple frowned. "What do you—"

"Everything OK in here?" asked a glamoured Mummy, joining them in the office.

"I was just introducing Mum to Ms Frumple," Theodora explained.

"Wonderful. Did you hand in your assignments? Good. And Ms Frumple," said Mummy, coming to stand on Theodora's other side, "in future, please call us directly if Theodora is late with any homework – especially that which, if missed, will result in multiple punishments. I must say, I'm surprised you didn't call in the first instance."

And although her tone was light, Theodora sensed an edge to Mummy's words. Ms Frumple must have too, for she said, "A small oversight." When neither Mummy nor Althea replied, Ms Frumple added, "It won't happen again."

"I know it won't," Mummy agreed. "Because then we would have no choice but to report you to the school governors for gross misconduct."

Ms Frumple glared at her, but wisely said nothing.

"Come, Theodora," Mummy said.

"Just a minute," said Althea. "Ms Frumple, given your failure to notify Mummy about Theodora's overdue assignment, it only seems fair that all associated punishments are expunged from her record."

"Now, see here—"

"Excellent point," Mummy cut in. "Ms Frumple, we'll await your letter confirming that Theodora's record has been revised. If we haven't heard from you by Friday..." She trailed off, letting the unspoken threat linger. "Do we understand one another?"

Two pink spots appeared on Ms Frumple's cheeks. She eyed Mummy with such loathing that Theodora thought her hatred of her might surpass even Hilda's. Nevertheless, she agreed with a short, sharp nod.

Theodora couldn't help grinning as they left the office; it was good to see Ms Frumple finally put in her place. Behind them, the door slammed shut with such force it made the glass in the windowpane rattle. This was followed by the unmistakable sound of paper being ripped.

"My poster," Theodora said sadly. "I wanted to hang that in my room..."

"We'll make another," Althea promised, "one that features the *whole* family, with pictures and everything. We can use some of the photos you took in New York!"

"We can make a night of it," said Mummy. "We'll order a pizza and I'll bake cupcakes. It'll be fun going through all the old photo albums – you were such a cute baby, Theodora."

"Incidentally, do vampires appear in photographs?" Althea wondered as they approached the Year Five classroom. "How about ghosts?"

The rest of the morning passed quickly, and before she knew it the lunch bell was ringing. Theodora and Dexter made their way to lunch, settling at their usual table. They were soon joined by Ella and Billy. Theodora should have known that her good mood was too good to last, for talk soon turned to Ella's party, which was coming up that weekend.

"I can't wait," said Billy, who was eating his lunch in reverse, having just taken a bite of his chocolate bar. (I like his style.) "Only, my dad says I have to bring my little brother cos he's got to go to work. That OK?"

Ella shrugged. "Sure. My grandpa always says the more the merrier."

This was too much for Theodora; it was one thing for her not to be invited to the party, but it was quite another for Ella to include someone she didn't even know.

Catching sight of Theodora's thunderous expression, Dexter asked, "Are you OK?"

"Yeah, what's up with you, Theo-*bora*?" grinned Billy, using his old nickname to tease her.

Theodora looked away. "Is that why you guys don't want to hang out with me?" she asked, picking at the bread of her sandwich. "Because I'm boring?"

"You're a lot of things, Theodora," Dexter exclaimed, "but boring isn't one of them!"

"Why would you think we didn't want to hang out with you?" asked Ella, carefully marking her place in her book before setting it aside.

Theodora finally looked up. "Because you didn't invite me to your party. You invited the whole class, even Billy's little brother – everyone except for me."

An awkward silence fell over the table. Dexter shifted uncomfortably in his seat, while Billy shoved the rest of his chocolate bar into his mouth just for something to do. Ella, though, slapped a hand against her forehead, then jumped up from the table and ran out of the lunch hall.

"That was weird," Billy said through a mouthful of chocolate. "Even for Ella."

Ella returned a few minutes later. "Here," she said breathlessly, pushing a crumpled envelope into Theodora's hand. "It's an invitation to my party."

Theodora blushed as violently as a sun-ripened strawberry. "You don't have to," she muttered. Somehow, being invited to the party because Ella felt guilt – or worse, pity – was even worse than not being invited at all.

"Look, it's yours – it's got your name on and everything! I handed these out right before the

Christmas break. You were in Ms Frumple's office at the time, I remember now. I meant to give you yours afterwards, but I forgot. It's been at the bottom of my knapsack since before the holidays."

Theodora felt something fluttering in her chest, as if a tiny dove was flapping its wings. "Really?" she asked.

"Really," Ella promised. "I'm so sorry I forgot. You must have felt awful!"

"I did," Theodora admitted. "But I should have said something."

"I wish you had. Oh, you *can* come, can't you? It won't be the same without you."

The dove in Theodora's chest soared. "Of course I can! Did you say there's going to be an ice cream bar?"

"Yes! And a magician, and games, and…"

And that, my friends, is the end of this long, spooky tale.

Almost.

EPILOGUE

New Beginnings

That Saturday, the day of Ella's party, was as cold as any in recent memory. A fresh coat of soft, powdery snow had blanketed the village, which looked like a scene on a postcard. The children of Appleton were taking full advantage of this, making snow angels, building snowmen, having snowball fights and catching snowflakes on their tongues until their parents yelled, "Come inside, it's time for cocoa!" Yes, all was well; the question, of course, was if it would remain so.

I am sorry to say that Hilda and the skele-crow have thus far evaded capture. They're out there somewhere, undoubtedly plotting their next attempt to bring monsters out of hiding. The London MLM deeply regret allowing them to escape (again), but as Wilhelmina said, there was no use crying over spilled potion.

I am *not* sorry to say that in light of recent events, the London MLM had formed a new division whose sole purpose was to locate and protect humans who could see through glamours: the Second Sight Squad. Althea, Mrs Adebola and Theodora (acting as a Junior Associate) were also members. They'd asked Ms Idris to join too, but she'd declined. The human squad members were planning another visit to New York City – now free of the fog that permeated its streets during the Shadowmongers' reign – to try to persuade her. Theodora was very excited by the prospect: she was eager to see Boolivia again, who'd been restored

to her former glory and who'd promised to take her to see the American Ballet Theatre as a thank you for defeating the Shadowmongers. And much to both Boolivia's and Theodora's delight, Gabe was even considering accompanying them.

I am pleased to say that *The Moon* card had stopped showing up in Theodora's daily torat spread the day after her nightmares ceased. And although the pack was now missing a card, it seemed to be functioning normally.

And I am delighted to say that Althea had settled right into life with the MLM. Though it felt a bit strange at times, Theodora was enjoying getting to know her second mother – or her first, I suppose (depending on how you look at it). After all these years, it was something of a relief to finally learn the truth about her origins, though Althea remained frustratingly opaque about Theodora's human father...

You're curious about that, too? I figured. Well, as a reward for all your hard work on this case, I'm going to tell you one last secret: I am Theodora's father.

Shocking, I know.

Yes, it was I who left Theodora in the Appleton graveyard so many years ago, trusting that Georgie and Bandit would discover her, hoping the MLM would raise her as their own. And so, they did! You're wondering why I haven't revealed myself to Theodora – especially now that Althea has returned? Alas, that's one secret I can't share – at least, not yet; timing is everything, you know.

And so, Junior Agent, our time together has come to an end. Or, perhaps I should say, *Agent* – look at you, promoted again! I feel certain you're ready to go out on your own ... unless you wanted to stay on with the Eye Spy Monster Agency? We offer a competitive salary, benefits and a generous year-end bonus (subject to performance review). Fair warning, though: if you accept, you'll be working long days and even longer nights. But in exchange, I'll promise you this: the quest – no, journey – no, adventure – of a lifetime. One filled with monsters and magic, excitement and danger – and, of course, friendship.

So, are you in?

ACKNOWLEDGEMENTS

First and foremost, thanks to my fabulous agent, Chloe Seager, for your support, your encouragement, and your love of all things spooky. You're amazing!

To the entire team at Walker Books: thank you – you're *fantastic*. Special thanks to my marvellous editor, Emma Lidbury, for your enthusiasm, your partnership, your thoughtful suggestions which *never* fail to improve my stories and, of course, your baking skills (I will never forget those bat cookies!); I am so very grateful. Huge thanks to Chloé Tartinville for the stunning design, to Jenny Bish for the exceptional copy edits, to Karen Coeman for the excellent work on foreign rights, and to Rebecca Oram for the terrific publicity.

To the fabulous Chris Jevons for the equally fabulous cover design and to the incredible Lisa Hunt for the exquisite interior illustrations, I thank you both.

To my lovely, wonderful friends who have cheered me on from the first to the last, thank you; it means more to me than you know. Special thanks to Sylwia Tyburska, without whose assistance this book would not have been finished on time, and to Bella Leone, reader extraordinaire: may you never lose your love of reading nor your independent spirit.

To my family: thank you for your unerring support and for providing me with a lifetime's worth of material (looking at you, Tappy Jordan, and you, Joseph Chilelli, and *you*, Barbara Kopyscianski). To my mother, Tamara Kopy Chilelli, who's been my biggest cheerleader from the moment I first put pen to paper (or fingertips to keyboard, as it were). To my beloved, late grandfather, Russell Kopyscianski, who would have been SO proud to see three of my books on his bookshelf. To my lovely in-laws, Peter and Tracie Coletto, for your kind words of encouragement. To Camy, my feline editor, for keeping my lap warm through those long, late-night writing sessions. And last but never least to my husband, Todd Patrick Coletto, for your brilliant insights, your remarkable patience, and your love; I am so lucky to call you mine and love you more than words can express.

And finally, to you, dear reader, for joining Theodora on all her adventures; I am so very humbled and grateful. Thank you one and all!

Jordan Kopy is a born and raised New Yorker who resides in London with her husband and poorly behaved (but loveable!) cat. A financial services professional by day, she spends her nights with ghouls, witches and the occasional evil hag. *Theodora Hendrix and the Snare of the Shadowmongers* is the third book in the Theodora Hendrix series, sequel to *Theodora Hendrix and the Monstrous League of Monsters* and *Theodora Hendrix and the Curious Case of the Cursed Beetle.* Jordan is currently writing a new contemporary fantasy novel for children.

Chris Jevons loved drawing from an early age, and after studying art, design and animation at university, he worked as a graphic designer and a 2D animator before pursuing a career in children's publishing. Chris illustrates picture books and fiction for a variety of publishers and lives and works in Harrogate.

Lisa Hunt has worked as an illustrator for over 15 years. Originally from Yorkshire, she now lives near London with her partner and their ginger cat.